Also by Pam Conrad

I DON'T LIVE HERE!

PRAIRIE SONGS

HOLDING ME HERE

WHAT I DID FOR ROMAN

SEVEN SILLY CIRCLES

STAYING NINE

MY DANIEL

Taking the Ferry Home

PAM CONRAD

HARPER & ROW, PUBLISHERS
Grand Rapids, Philadelphia, St. Louis, San Francisco,
London, Singapore, Sydney, Tokyo
NEW YORK

Typography by Albert Cetta
2   3   4   5   6   7   8   9   10

Library of Congress Cataloging-in-Publication Data
Conrad, Pam.
    Taking the ferry home.

    Summary: Two sixteen-year-old girls from different
social classes spend the summer together on a resort
island and experience a test of their friendship
when family loyalties, romance, and drug dependence
interfere.
    [1. Friendship—Fiction.   2. Family problems—Fiction]
I. Title.
PZ7.C76476Tak 1988   [Fic]   87-45856
ISBN 0-06-021317-5
ISBN 0-06-021318-3 (lib. bdg.)

for Carole Gleason Crowe
on the *Morning Dove*

Taking the Ferry Home

Ali

I probably would have met her sooner or later that summer, since my father's rented cottage was right near her parents' mansion, but as it happened I met her that very first night. I can still remember when I saw her sitting there alone in the late-summer darkness, and I guess I sensed even then that there was something very unsettling about Simone Silver.

She was the kind of girl every guy in the world would fall in love with. Fall in love with, and then never get up the courage to talk to, she seemed so unapproachable. I met her that first night while sneaking a swim in her pool. The moon was so bright that I remember being surprised by the crisp clear shadow I cast before me as I crept over the dark summer lawn.

Daddy had taken me there earlier that day. We weren't really supposed to be there then either, but he had said that in broad daylight it didn't count as trespassing, especially since no one had arrived there yet for the summer. He had shown me the elaborate garden, the flowers arranged in patterns that seemed so natural yet must have been carefully thought out, the brick walkways, the smooth wooden deck. Even the weeping willows in the background seemed to have been carefully placed. The sun had glinted off the white shades that hung down one side of the white gazebo. Behind us was the tennis court, and beyond the pool—its edge seeming to rise into the sky—was the bay, so blue I could have tasted it.

"I don't believe this," I had whispered to my father. "This is outrageous. Can you imagine what it must be like to *live* in a place like this? Where are the owners?"

"Still in the city," he answered. "This is their *summer place.*"

Summer place. I had walked over to the tremendous pool and placed the toes of my running shoes along its edge. In the daylight it had looked like a cool forest kind of pool, as if it had just appeared naturally. Along the sides bubbles rose from a silent filter.

"It's heated, too," Daddy added, smiling at me. Playfully he had clasped my elbow and pretended he was going to push me in. I didn't laugh.

"But doesn't this make you depressed? To see that some people live like this?" I waved my arm around at the whole scene. "I mean, couldn't you just die for this? It's not fair. *You* deserve a place like this, and not just for weekends, or the summer, but for all the time."

He tugged at my long braid and walked away from me. When I turned he was sitting on a stone garden seat, a long wooden bench held up on both sides by the heads of two sulking child angels. He slipped his bare feet from his old moccasins and rubbed his soles over the grass. "I make myself rich by making my wants few," he quoted. "Besides, a place like this is a lot of work and a lot of headaches. You've got to vacuum the pool all the time with these trees around, varnish the deck every year, weed the garden, keep the birdbath full."

"Gimme a break," I moaned, collapsing beside him on the bench. "I bet these people never do any of that stuff. They pay someone to do it. While they're not looking."

"I did meet the caretaker," he admitted. "Larsen, a nice old guy. He told me I could do a few laps in the mornings when no one was around. But that was last month, before the season. I keep worrying they'll be here soon, so I haven't been coming over. No one here yet, though," he remarked, looking toward the house, a large white Victorian with a porch that wrapped around the bay side. There wasn't a soul around.

That's what had given me the idea to sneak over and use the pool myself, in the dark, once Daddy'd gone off to one of his meetings. In the light of the moon, I crept across the Silvers' lawn, the large house looming dark, the frogs singing in the bushes. I slipped off my clogs and placed them beside my towel at the edge of the pool. I was wearing my varsity-team bathing suit, an ugly blue-and-orange Olympic-type thing. As quietly as I could, without disturbing the surface, I slid into the water. It was as warm as the air, and I was buoyant and free. I sank into it, letting it rise above my head, and kicking off from the side, I swam under the surface the full length of the pool. Reaching the other side, I caught my breath and began an easy crawl across the surface, one lap side crawl, one lap backstroke, one lap breaststroke, back and forth, tiring myself, until at last I just hovered near the deep end, treading water and smiling into the starry darkness. It was then that I saw her.

She was sitting quietly on a padded lawn chair right in front of me. Her legs were crossed Indian fashion beneath her, and her wrists were resting on her knees like some kind of guru's. Her hair draped over her shoulders and shone black against her skin. "Are you through?" she asked.

I kept treading and watching her. " 'Scuse me?" I asked, stalling for time.

"I said are you through trespassing?"

"I guess I am," I said, searching for my towel. I swam over to it, but my arms were so weak from my laps, I couldn't lift myself out of the water. I tried to hoist myself up two or three times, and then swam to the ladder and dragged myself out. The air suddenly felt very cool.

I reached for my towel, feeling ridiculous in my team bathing suit. She was wearing a small bikini that looked shimmery in the darkness. I rubbed myself down, trembling and chilly, feeling foolish.

"Are you one of the waitresses from the Pridley?" she asked coolly.

The Pridley was the island's exclusive hotel, where the

sub-elite stayed, the wealthy summer islanders who didn't own summer houses. I immediately got an attitude, even though my mother had suggested that very thing to me, that I get a job there this summer.

"No," I answered just as coolly. "I'm staying with my father in our cottage across the way."

"Across *what* way?" she asked. She looked like she was sixteen or seventeen, about my age, yet she was lighting a cigarette as if she were an actress, or maybe a child pretending, and I could see in the match light a slight smirk spread across her face. She shook the match with manicured nails, maybe even fake nails, and she blew a stream of smoke into the air and waited.

I motioned with my head toward our cottage.

"That's *my* cottage," she stated.

"Right," I answered. I tossed the towel over my shoulders. Daddy had told me it belonged to the owners of this house. It had been the servants' quarters once. I remembered now. I was half waiting to be dismissed, or for her to call someone to take me away in shackles. I don't know, but I didn't feel like I could just walk away. "Listen," I said, "sorry about the—"

"Your father is the writer?" she interrupted, and then she held out her pack of cigarettes. "Have one?"

I shook my head at the cigarettes. "Yes, Charlie Mintz, that's my father, the one and only."

"Charlie!" she laughed. "You always hear it Charles. Charles A. Mintz it says in *The New York Times* this week.

My father is beside himself, you know. He'll only rent to status folk. He'd rather let it sit empty all year than rent it to just anybody. And where's your mother? What does she do?"

"Listen," I said, irritated now. I always hated it when people fawned over my father. Was that why my father had been able to get the cottage? Because he was chic to be around? "I'm done trespassing. Can I go home now to *your* cottage? Or do you have to interrogate me first?"

Her laughter was loud and almost catching. I bit the inside of my lip and frowned at her.

"Come on," she prodded. "Relax. I'm Simone Silver. You've probably heard about me. Reigning princess of Dune Island."

I couldn't tell in the dark if she was being sarcastic or not, but by the sound of her voice, I had the queer feeling she was dead serious, devoid of pride or grandiosity, just bluntly stating the facts. But she was wrong. I hadn't heard about her at all.

"Princess?" I hissed sarcastically. "I thought Dune Island was part of America. Have I missed something?"

"Look around you—what's your name?"

"Ali."

"Look around you, Ali. Royal gardens or what?" She waved her arm around the gardens, which were lit with electric lanterns in the shrubbery. "And when your father is king, and your mother is queen"—there was an edge of bitterness to her voice now—"that makes you a princess, like it or not."

"And you don't love it," I said, challenging the part of her that sounded almost human.

"I love it," she said, standing and tossing her cigarette behind her onto the lawn.

For an instant I hated her for no other reason than she was beautiful, completely beautiful, and she wasn't even nice. I twitched with the unfairness of it. After all, I was so nice. She poised herself on the edge of the pool, lean and perfectly proportioned as if money had not only straightened her teeth and buffed her skin, but had also lengthened her thighs and shaped her torso. She would be the girl who always got the guy, the older man, the richer man, the rock star. And then without a splash or a sound she disappeared into the water.

In an instant she came up furious. "Jesus, why does Larsen keep this so warm? It's a bathtub." She splashed like a mermaid, sending a spray of water around herself, and she shook her head almost in slow motion so her hair fanned out above the water, sending beads of light all over. Choked with jealousy, I turned and, without a word, made my way back over the lawn, careful of the cigarette that glowed like a fallen star chip in the grass.

Simone

I wonder. I wonder.

I look in the mirror and watch my hair fly about my head in the hot air as I dry it. I stare into my eyes, beyond my eyes, and I wonder. About her. Her father, her mother, about what it's like in that cottage now with them in there—a writer, a girl my age. She seemed so touchy, uneasy. I'll have to go slow with her, take my time. Or I might be alone all summer again, with no one to take off with, no one to be my excuse for never being around.

I hate being here like this, in my room, stuck in this moment. I want to fly ahead and see what will happen, fly behind and see what's gone on. Be everywhere, every-time, all ways. But I'm just Simone, stuck in my life, stuck right here when I could scream to be anywhere else, even to be *someone* else—even that girl. To be her and to stay in the cottage, Adilia's old cottage.

I turn the hair blower off. I hate the silence. My windows look out into darkness. Larsen must have turned off the pool lights already. The other window looks out onto the inland water. It is dark, black, a light or two flickering in the trees. I think how I have never been so lonely, and then I hear footsteps in the hall and freeze. Did I lock it? Did I remember?

Something rubs against my door. "Simone, dear? Are you awake?"

I don't answer. The doorknob turns only so far. It is locked. I can feel myself relax now. Mother wants to talk, to stretch out on my bed with her tinkling glass in her hand and tell me about her childhood, about my father, her father, about what to watch out for in life. She wants to talk on and on until she falls asleep on my bed, limp and snoring. And I'll have to find somewhere else to go, or call Father to come and get her.

But the door is locked. I am sleeping, Mother, I say silently.

"I know you're not sleeping," she says, as if she reads my mind. "I heard your hair dryer just a moment ago."

But I say nothing.

"Simone. I'd like to talk to you. Simone?" She sounds as if she might cry.

I am braced against it.

"Simone?" And then I hear in the deepest, quietest voice what I've known all along. "You little brat." And she moves away from the door and down the hall.

My life is like a movie, I think. A thriller, and this is the part where everyone takes a deep breath. I put her from my mind like turning off the hot smoky light in a projector. She's gone. Out of my mind. And all that's left is a kind of strange exhilaration.

What now? I walk around my room. It's been a long time since I've been here, since last summer. I forget how it looks, how it feels, and now, standing in my room again, it's like I've never been gone. Crates of my clothes are still piled in the corner. Ramona will put them away tomorrow for me. I open the closet door and look inside. Here are the things I leave here, things that wait for me, that never change, things that witness my changes.

I hesitate and then toss the large pink lion onto my bed. What the hell? I slip my feet into the dark-blue clogs. I still like them. I touch the sleeves of a terry beach coat, ugly, and pull down a straw hat with ribbon streamers and little flowers on the crown. I tug at a scarf, and it draws something heavy across the shelf. Instantly I remember—Adilia's old tarot cards. She kept them wrapped in a silk scarf, and I took them from her cottage that last summer.

Adilia. How exotic she was to me when I was little, with her lilting voice thick with her native patois, and how brown she was. I was sure then that if I had dared to put her finger in my mouth, she would have tasted like gingerbread. Now I hold her cards in my hand. I used to watch her lay them out, study them, read them, but it's been so long.

Have I forgotten all she taught me? What was it she

said to do first, before reading them? Before even looking at them? I know now. I must wrap them in silk and sleep with them under my pillow. Then they will speak to me. I see her dark fingers winding the scarf around them. I do it now. It makes a soft and heavy package in my hands.

I close the closet door and carry the cards across the room to my bed. Gently, I place them under my pillow. But I am not ready for sleep yet. Mother is gone. The hall light is out beneath my door. I'll play some tapes. Some Springsteen maybe. And wait.

Ali

When I got back to the cottage that night, only Lois, my father's golden retriever, was there. She was sleeping in the doorway between the kitchen and the living room, and she lifted her head to see who it was. When she saw me, her face spread into what my mother liked to call a smile and her head dropped back down on her front paws with a sigh. Daddy hadn't come home yet, and my mother wasn't due out for a while. This was my first unstructured summer, no summer school of flute practice, no day camp or lifeguard instruction or miles of lanyards, no sleepaway camps of hot bunks and soggy spaghetti. Just sweet summer days of unstructured, unbordered, undisciplined hours of time.

I had fantasies of a summer romance, a lifeguard who read books or a young vacationing college student looking for an honest woman. I had promised everyone that I wouldn't interfere with Daddy's work. I would make him lunch each day if he wanted and keep out of his way. I was old enough to be on my own without chaperones, counselors, or watchdogs. "You'll be bored out of your mind," my mother had warned me. "You'd better get a job at the Pridley or something." But Daddy had understood. It was fine with him. He didn't mind having me around. And it was cheaper than camp.

The cottage had its own peculiar smell, like wood and ocean, bug spray and towels. I pulled the string over the kitchen table and the room blasted to life around me. I didn't like how the place looked at night, with the dark windows, and with no curtains or shades. The wood-paneled walls that looked so nice and warm in the daylight, looked depressing and poor at night. Or was it just that I had spent a few too many minutes poolside with the "princess of Dune Island"?

"Ha!" I said right out loud, searching the shelves of the refrigerator. "And I guess that makes me the court jester's daughter." I slammed a heavy glass on the table and filled it with iced tea. Not the greatest choice for bedtime, but I didn't care. I didn't have to get up any special time, didn't have to get my rest or sleep soundly. Actually, I even thought of staying up all night, so I wouldn't miss a thing that first night.

I climbed the ladder-stairs to the loft, my room for the summer. It promised to be hot and stuffy with its two tiny windows, the only ones in the whole cottage that had curtains. They looked like they'd let in about as much air as kitten lungs. I dropped my wet bathing suit to my ankles and kicked it aside. If I'd been home, I would have examined myself in my full-length mirror, to check and see in exactly what ways I was not at all like her highness, but there was no mirror here. So why did I have to look at myself? I knew I didn't compare. My wet braid lay down the length of my back the color and heft of a tugboat rope, and where her legs and torso had been streamlined, mine were muscular. I was definitely the sidekick type.

I slipped my nightgown on. I pulled my hair out of its braid and toweled it. I grew dizzy with my own roughness and finally sat on the straw rug on the floor, tossing the towel aside. With my hair like brambles and my jaw already too tight, I made myself sit up straight. I crossed my legs Indian fashion beneath me and rested my wrists on my knees like a guru. I tried to feel it—what it must be like to be her. But I knew my ankles were scraped, my face was splotchy and flushed, and my nails were bit to the quick. I didn't move.

I just sat there, my hair dripping down my back, my thigh muscles aching, my nails growing ever so slowly on the tips of my fingers. Enough. Enough self-pity. No sulking this summer. Like a ghost slipping out of its earthly body, I left the image of Simone Silver there on the floor and, rousing myself, padded back down the ladder-stairs.

The cottage had an old porch around two sides of it, an extra room that was all screen and air. I lit a small lamp near the sofa and looked around at the old wicker furniture, dark green and scratchy. The chairs and the sofa had cushions that felt like they were stuffed with straw, but they were comfortable. I sank into the sofa, squirming and adjusting till a nest formed around me. I had brought my book, my iced tea; and with Simone temporarily released from my mind and body, I was perfectly content. The lamp drew a circle around the pages of my book, and despite the iced tea, my eyes grew heavy and I faded out.

I don't know how long I had been sleeping, but I woke to hear voices. I knew my father's routine. He was sitting in a car near the cottage, talking. I didn't know his friends on the island yet, but I heard a voice that sounded as if it had been bottled in Brooklyn, and a laugh that was deep and rough. He always did this after his AA meetings, carried on the talk, drew it out, like humming a Broadway tune when you leave the theater. He took it with him. Made it last.

I willed myself to stay sleeping. I didn't move. Lois trotted onto the porch fully awake and excited. Through heavy eyes, I watched her press her nose to the screen and moan a long, slow woof. I could hear the car door open and good-nights exchanged. The car rolled back out the drive, sending beams of light across the porch. Lois ran from the porch to the back door, where I could hear my father rough her up, love her. "Howrya doin', old girl, huh? Keeping an eye on things, are you?" He spoke loudly, but his voice dipped to a whisper as he stepped out into the lit porch and saw me there.

"Shhh, now," he said to her. I heard him pat her hollow-sounding chest. I expected him to ruffle my hair, shake me, and tell me to move on up to my own bed. I hung precariously on that edge of sleep and wakefulness, waiting for him. I heard him click out the light. I opened one sleepy eye and saw him looking out into the night with Lois' head pressed against his leg. He was very still and quiet; my eyes closed. I forgot he was there until I felt him cover me with an afghan and leave me there to sleep.

I listened to his footsteps through the cottage. The bath-room door, the water running, the sound of his mattress creaking, his shoes dropping. And even though my body was asleep, my mind was sharp. I heard every sound, felt every inch of my body, smelled the honeysuckle, felt the warmth behind my knees, and then from across the road heard Bruce Springsteen calling to me, telling me about a love he'd lost, and I thought with a familiar tugging, "Oh, yes, that's what I want—a love, even a sad love, even if I have to lose it. I want a sad love this summer."

Simone

The morning dew soaks into my running shoes, making them dark and heavy. I carry his book. Maybe he will sign it. Maybe she will be there, and she'll go running with me. If I promise to show her the small pier along the road, that juts out into the water, maybe then she'll come.

I am tall now. I can feel it. The distance between the big house and the cottage is not so great anymore, not like it once was, when I would run and run and run and still not be there. Now I feel my legs, long and lean striding across the wet lawn. I needn't run. I must remember I am really this big, this grown. That I can do anything I want. I wish Adilia could see me now. There is nothing I can't have. Nothing that won't come to me if I wish it.

The cottage is quiet. The storm door is closed behind the screen door. No one is up yet. When Adilia lived here, she never locked the doors, and she would always come across the lawn early in the morning singing her West Indian songs, swinging one massive leg in front of the other. I would lie in bed, hiding, and when I heard her coming, I would come down. It was good when she was here. And then there were the few mornings when I got up first and went to her, like this, running as much away from the big house as toward her. I must have been seven. Had it really begun that long ago? Had Mother's drinking been bad then, too? I don't remember. I only remember running from her. I remember Adilia's fat warm lap, and her kissing lips in my hair, and her comforting arms all about me. Today the cottage is locked. Charles A. Mintz is here. And that girl.

The hollyhocks are coming up on either side of the locked door, reminding me of how Adilia used to keep witchcraft things in the cottage, things she'd sweep off the table and bury out of sight when I came in. But I knew there was mystery and power in her little locks of hair and pieces of root and candles. One morning I brought her hollyhock flowers, from right outside her door where we had planted them together. I tore them off their long hairy stems and presented them to her, my arms covered with their pollen like Parmesan cheese.

She had put the flowers in a jar and scraped the pollen off my arms with a matchbook, collecting it in her hand. "Hollyhock powder is magic, chile," she told me. "We mustn't waste it." She made a little pyramid of it on the kitchen table and sat looking at it. "You can make a wish now," she told me, smoothing her big brown hand up my arm. "Make a wish," she urged, and she spread my fingers out on the table so my two thumbs were pointing to the pyramid.

I remember the quiet, the warmth of her kitchen, the sound of her breathing. "I wish Adilia was my mother," I said to the pile of hollyhock powder.

"No, no, no, chile. Not that kind of wish that cannot come true. You have a mother. I tell you, make a wish that holds possibilities."

A wish that holds possibilities. I thought of my mother and her pearl necklace that she'd grip if I came near, the stiff hair that would back away from me if I tried to put my arm around her neck. I wasn't sure what possibilities were there at all.

Adilia straightened my fingers again, aligning them with powder and north and west. "Come, now, a wish. Before it dries and loses its power."

"I wish my mother had a big fat lap," I whispered to the pyramid.

Adilia scooped the powder onto the matchbook then and poured it into my hand. "Good," she said, "and now, when your mother is not looking, put this powder in her pockets. Go along now. I will come up to the house as soon as I can. You wait there for me."

I couldn't put the powder in Mother's pockets. She didn't have pockets that I could see in her linen suit, and she was all alert and nervous, watching me every minute if I was in the room with her. I think I sprinkled it in her pocketbook that sat on the front hall table. All day I had carried the stain on my palm.

And she never had any kind of lap for me.

The door suddenly unlocks and a large golden dog pushes the screen door open. A man stands in the doorway in jeans and a flannel shirt. He's very nice-looking, not handsome really, but attractive, alert. He has a mug in his hand and he's looking at me. Here is Charles A. Mintz. His photograph fills the back cover of the book I have in my hand. I could hold it up next to his head, and it would be the exact face, only behind the screen he looks a little startled and uncertain.

"Good morning, Mr. Mintz," I say, extending my hand to him in front of the screen door. I am surprised at my voice. I sound like my mother. Have I developed that, or is it just inherited vocal cords and lips muscles?

He opens the door and switching the mug to his left hand, he shakes hands with me. He doesn't know what I'm doing here.

"I'm Simone Silver. I'm glad you're up so early. I was hoping to catch you before you began work. My father says you're working on a new novel." I keep my face open. I tap the book in my hand. "I was hoping to get an autograph."

"You caught me just in time," he says. He motions for me to come into the kitchen. "Have a seat. I'll get my pen."

There's a pile of books on the table, a dirty cereal bowl with blue milk left in it, and a jar of vitamins. He roots around the table, looking for his pen.

"It's too bad my daughter's not awake yet. You two should meet. You're probably around the same age."

"We've met," I tell him, but not how. "I was wondering also if she'd like to go for a jog. I run every morning."

He slips the book from my hands and sits across the table. He is studying me. "Have you read this?" he asks, with a questioning kind of grin. "I can't get Ali to read it. It's probably just as well," he mutters. "S-i-m-o-n-e?" he asks. I nod and he bends over the book. He forgets he asked me if I've read it, and I don't tell him I haven't, that it's my father's.

There's a noise behind us and we both turn to see the girl in the doorway with an afghan around her shoulders like an old squaw. She is standing there glaring at me.

"Here she is now," Charles A. Mintz says. "Well, how'd you sleep, Pepper? I didn't have the heart to move you last night, you looked so comfy." He's smiling at her. I look from her to him, watching how they do this. I smile at her too. She doesn't smile. She's just standing there, waiting.

"Your father is autographing a copy of his book for me," I tell her.

"So that's it," she mumbles.

"And I was wondering if you wanted to jog this morning. I run every morning, before it gets too hot."

She doesn't answer. I could almost climb up on the chair for wanting to try harder, but I keep cool, slow. "I'm on the cross-country team up at school, and I need to keep running this summer."

"Why don't you go, Ali?" Charles A. Mintz says. He begins to clear the table. He suddenly seems finished with me, eager for Ali to take over. Maybe he wants to get to his work.

"I just got up." She is whining. "I didn't even shower yet."

"Just get your sweats on," I tell her, pretending I'm reading the inscription in her father's book. "Shower when we get back." *For Simone Silver, May this be a memorable summer. Charles A. Mintz*

"Well, see you girls later," her father says, passing her in the doorway. "It was nice meeting you, Simone," he says politely to me. And to his daughter, "Have a good run." He kisses her cheek, like some fathers do. And he's gone. The girl and I are alone in the kitchen together. She is glaring at me. I look back at her. I have to be kinder.

"Oh, and Ali?" he calls from another room. "I'll be going to an afternoon meeting with someone around one. Just in case you're looking for me." And he's gone. I hear a door close.

"What kind of meeting?" I ask, nosy and for something to say.

"I don't know." I can tell she's lying. She doesn't want to talk about it. She wants me to leave, but I won't, not yet.

"So, will you run? Around the inland waters, about

four miles. There's a nice pier I'll show you. And a beach where everyone goes."

She stares at me, through me.

"Give me a few minutes," she says.

She'll come. She'll come. I nod and sit back in the wooden chair. I drum my fingernails on her father's book. I am too nervous waiting in the kitchen. Adilia's kitchen. I have to wait outside. The dog is sitting on the back step, staring into the distance. It ignores me.

When the girl comes out, I show her the hollyhocks. "I planted these once," I tell her. "Maybe ten years ago. We had a Jamaican servant who showed me how." I see the seeds held in Adilia's dark fingers that are worn black around her joints. She is chanting, *One to rot, one to grow, one for the pigeon, and one for the crow.* I tell the girl, "They'll be lovely by July."

"You have servants?" she asks. I can hear a tightness in her voice and feel myself pull in, like the living pulp in a conch shell.

"Many," I answer, beginning to jog toward the road, easy, loping. I can hear her running to my side and slightly behind, picking up my stride immediately. "That particular one was a fat West Indian woman. I forget her name."

Ali

What . . . a . . . snot, I thought. What was I doing? I had a million things I'd rather be doing, like flossing my teeth, cleaning out the car, having diarrhea, and here I was running after the princess of Dune Island along one of her majesty's quiet roads, like some kind of handmaiden, one of her ladies-in-waiting. And she didn't have the courtesy to pace herself down a little. I had the distinct impression she was even trying to lose me. She took long steady strides, and I tried to match her. Soon we settled into a rhythm, three of my steps to two of hers, and while her breathing seemed effortless, I had to think out every breath, pace, pace, and hope that my lungs didn't start whistling Dixie.

Just when I thought I couldn't go another step, and was about to duck into the brush on the side of the road and let her think she'd lost me, she headed up a dirt path. It was as if she had turned off a switch. She instantly changed her pace and walked slowly and deliberately up the path. Like a fighter, I kept running in place, cooling down, two paces behind her. My T-shirt was sopping and sticking to me. I noticed a delicate cross of perspiration across her shoulders and down the center of her back. Ahead of me, she smelled like lily of the valley. I wiped my face across my T-shirt sleeve and sweat dripped off my elbow.

"Here's the pier I told you about," she said. She acted as if it were some kind of gift she was giving me. "The best view on the island," she said. She sat down right on the edge, her legs dangling. Mindful of the sea-gull droppings, I sat gingerly beside her, the soles of my running shoes just touching the surface of the calm water. "Father wants to get me a small motor boat this summer," she said. "I'd keep it right here. This is perfect."

She looked at me, for a reaction I guess, and then just stared.

"What's the matter?" I asked her.

"Your face is bright red. Are you all right?"

I cupped my hands over my cheeks. Tried to regulate my voice and my breath now. "Sure. I just get flushed easily when I run."

"You should've said something. Were we going too fast?"

"I said I was fine."

"Sometimes I forget. It's like I get high and just keep going faster and farther. I started running soon after my skiing accident in Switzerland a couple of years ago."

"You had a skiing accident?"

"Yes. Broke my leg in three places. The doctors said I'd never walk again."

I looked down at her leg there on the pier. Long, pale, a perfectly perfect leg. "Jeez. Was it painful?"

"Sure. A cast from here to here. Then crutches, a cane. They couldn't keep me down, though. In a year, I was walking three miles a day, and soon after that, I was running parts of it. Haven't stopped since. Nobody tells Simone Silver what she can and can't do."

I looked at her squinting off into the bay. She shaded her eyes with her hand, and I felt a faint stirring of admiration. This was no slouch rich kid. There might be something here. She was pointing, smiling. "Oh, look! Here they come!"

Off in the distance, coming around a turn in the inland water, was a small motorboat trailing a water-skier. I could hear the engine, soft as a fly, and see waves of spray first to the left, then the right of the skier. "The Pridley boat," she told me. "It's too early in the morning for the hotel guests to be out. It must be some of the staff. Wait till you see. They get the most gorgeous guys there in the summer."

The boat was swerving, and now I could hear the laughter. A cowboy whoop. I smoothed back my hair and plucked my wet T-shirt from my clammy ribs. Next to me, Simone pulled the elastic out of her hair, and her dark hair fell like ribbons over her shoulders. She had no makeup on, but she glowed anyway. We waited, sitting there on the end of the pier, the two of us jutting out into the water like brass rings waiting to be plucked. I would have given anything for a dry set of clothes.

There were two guys in the boat. One was sitting, and the other was standing at the wheel. The one at the wheel was bare chested and the color of coffee and cream. The guy being pulled was dark and muscular and had a thick mustache. The boat grew louder and louder. They drew close but hadn't seen us yet.

"See what I mean?" she whispered. She tilted my way and leaned against my shoulder slightly. "Pick one," she said.

I stopped breathing. What did she mean? I felt I was in F.A.O. Schwarz with a little rich girl who swept her arm across the doll wall and said, "Okay, which one do you want?"

"What do you mean, 'pick one'?" I couldn't take my eyes off them.

"Which one do you like the best? Go ahead! You can always change your mind later. But get started. Give yourself something to think about."

The guys in the boat saw us now, and without stopping they sped around and past the pier. Their faces were turned toward us. I looked from one to the other, the one sitting with a white T-shirt, blond, quiet-looking, the one being pulled behind, muscular, older, and the driver, his shoulders and chest bare, and now I could see he wore dark-blue bathing trunks. He was the one. I'll take that one, I told myself. But for Simone, I shrugged. They sped past.

"I don't know," I told her.

"The one with the mustache is cute," she said. I was surprised. I would have thought anyone less than a movie star wouldn't have interested the high-and-mighty Simone Silver. "So which one?" she pressed.

They were circling around, coming past us again. The guy in the white T-shirt leaned over toward our side of the boat. The one being pulled did a tiny leap and rode past us backward, the rope clasped behind him, and the driver smiled and lifted his hand in a wave. He smiled. Yes, that's the one, I thought. I felt Simone looking at me.

"The driver," she said immediately.

"I can tell," she said. "He's definitely your type. And he was looking at you. There's something cooking there. I just know it."

The boat zigzagged in the water, a cowboy whoop shot into the air, and they all disappeared back from where they had come, along the water through the marshes. It was suddenly very quiet. I tapped my feet on the water.

"So tomorrow we'll go down to the Pridley. Check him out for you." She sounded so sure of herself.

"What about you? Which one are you picking?" I was feeling defensive, as if she were taking over my life.

"None of them really interests me right now. I've had enough men for a while. I think I'll take a rest this summer."

Oh, give me a break.

"Okay, so it's tomorrow," she said. "At noon. We'll go for a swim at the Pridley beach."

"So what are you now, my camp counselor? Are you arranging my summer activities all of a sudden?"

She had such a nice smile, though, this girl who knew what she wanted and knew how to get it. She was grinning at me. Perfect teeth. "Well? Did you have some big plans?" she asked. "What were you going to do tomorrow? Brush your dog? Read a book?"

My nose twitched. She should only know. "But why tomorrow? Why not today?" I asked.

"I'm busy today," she said. She suddenly stood and brushed off the seat of her running shorts. "Mick Jagger is coming for lunch, and he always stays late." She turned and began jogging up the pier. I laughed out loud. I could have stayed right there that morning and let her run right out of my simple life with her silly pretensions and her snotty attitude, but I wasn't sure how to get back to the cottage. I hoisted myself up and took off after her, my calves screaming for mercy the minute my feet touched solid ground.

Simone

I have a friend. I say this to myself as we run along the roads through the hills. I must just be careful. I must keep her somehow. Let her know how good it will be to be my friend. I wonder if she drives. Maybe she'd like to drive Father's old Porsche. I'm going too fast again. I slow my pace, and we are quiet with each other. She bought that story about the ski accident. It wasn't really a lie. I never broke my leg, but if I did, that's how I'd be—determined, strong willed, back on my feet no matter what the doctors said. It is hard up these hills, but she doesn't complain. And I don't let on that a knife is driving into my lower ribs. I see the house up ahead. Maybe she will come in with me. I'll have Ramona fix us breakfast.

We come to the garden first and stop running. I walk along the border, and she is behind me running in place, puffing and panting. I motion her to follow me and she does. She is flushed again, and breathing hard.

"Do you like herb gardens?" I ask.

She shrugs.

"Look," I show her. I rub my fingers on the new basil

plants and bring my hand to her face. She smells my fingers and nods.

"Nice."

"And this is fennel," I tell her. Larsen has put a little sign beside each herb. This one says, "Sow fennel, sow sorrow." I don't tell her how Adilia once told me that fennel is the symbol of flattery, carried once by those who wished their insincere words to be accepted without distrust. I don't tell her, and I take a light feathery stem and twist it once through the loose weave of my shirt. It hangs like an Indian feather, and unknowing, she cuts a stem for herself and does the same.

"It grows by the sea," I say. "I knew someone once who hung sprigs of it over her door the night of the summer solstice to ward off evil spirits." Adilia balanced on a low milking stool and pressed a thumbtack into the molding of the doorway. The sprigs rained dried dusty feathers on anyone walking in and out the door. Even now the strong aroma, almost like dill, fills my head, and I ache.

"What is that?" she asks curiously, but I know she knows.

"Mother's marijuana," I say. And I turn away, but she stays there staring.

"All that? All that? Marijuana? Just growing here? Right out in the open?"

God, she is dumb. "It's not exactly out in the open. It's set back. Nobody comes up this way, unless they're coming to the house. It's no big deal."

"What does she do with it?"

Jesus. "She photographs it."

The girl looks at me. Her eyes probe into my head and she knows I'm being sarcastic. I don't want to talk about this anymore. I suddenly want her to go home. But she follows me up to the house.

"There's a shower there in the cabana," I tell her. "Why don't you take a shower there? I'll take one inside."

She agrees.

Inside, Mother is sitting at the kitchen table. I can tell she's hyper. She's got two newspapers spread out across the table and two cigarettes going.

"Darling! You're up and out so early," she says. She puts out her arm to me, and dutifully I lean toward her dry kiss that lands in the air by my ear. "And you look so healthy and luscious. All you need now is a tan." She goes back to the paper.

Ramona moves around by the stove, discreet and almost two-dimensional. "Would you like breakfast now, Miss Simone?" she asks.

"I'm taking a shower first, Ramona, then I'll have breakfast in the gazebo with my friend. She's showering in the cabana."

"A friend? A friend?" My mother jumps from her seat and peers out the window. "Who is she?"

She's so strung out. Maybe I should have told Ali to just go home. "Oh, nobody. The girl from the cottage. You know, the writer's daughter."

"What writer's daughter?"

"Mother! You know. In the cottage. Father rented the cottage to Charles A. Mintz. It's his daughter." I want to strangle her.

"Charles A. Mintz?" she whispers. "He's renting the cottage? *The* Charles A. Mintz?"

"You knew that, Mother. Father was just talking about it a couple of nights ago."

"Well," she says, "we must have them for dinner. A writer! A real writer!" She turns suddenly to Ramona. "I've heard writers are big drinkers, Ramona. Put in another order up at the Davis shop. More bourbon and scotch. We're low. And some of that nice wine. . . ."

I leave the room. I never should have mentioned it.

When I'm done with my shower, I find Ali in the gazebo. She has a thick towel around her head, and she is draping strips of lox over her bagel. Ramona has set out a tray of food and fruit that glistens in the sunlight.

"Wherever do you find lox on Dune Island?" Ali asks, taking a bite and staring at me with huge eyes.

"We have it sent in from the city."

She sighs with contentment and leans back in her seat.

"My mother didn't come out to talk to you, did she?" I ask.

"That wasn't your mother who brought out the tray and disappeared back into the house like a mouse, was it?"

"Hardly. My mother has never carried a tray in her life, and she never disappears like a mouse. More like a whale."

"What?"

"When she disappears, it's like a whale submerging. You never know where she'll burst out next, or what kind of mood she'll be in."

Ali looks kind of blank. "Yeah, mothers are something."

"She wants to invite your father and you, mostly your father, over for dinner. She's in there scurrying around, brushing up on her literary references and stocking up the liquor cabinet."

"Daddy doesn't drink," she says. "And he doesn't do anything social while he's working on a book."

"Doesn't drink?" How strange. "At all?"

"At all. But I'll come." She stands looking at the house. I know she's curious. Interested, even if she is acting a bit superior. "And I can talk literary if that's what she wants—symbolism, plot, pathos, limericks. You name it." Thoughtfully, facing the house, she begins to dry her hair. She wants to see inside. She wants to meet my mother. She would be surprised.

"What does *your* mother do?" I ask.

"Oh, she'll be out here soon. In a week or so. She's working on her doctorate. She's impossible to live with. She's a wreck." But Ali is smiling. It's probably not so bad.

"Can I braid your hair?" I ask suddenly. Her hair is long and thick. I can see it already in a French braid hugging the back of her head. It would be pretty.

She looks at me then. And I can see distrust waver over her like heat off an asphalt road. "Why?"

I shrug. "I like to braid."

A window slides up at the house. And then another as Ramona moves through the rooms. Out on the bay I can see a sailboat sitting very still, its sails limp. A bee hovers an instant by my foot and then moves on. I wait.

"Okay," she says, as if she's made a decision. And she sits herself in the chair by my side.

Ali

It looked like there had been a vegetable garden or something beside our cottage once. Long ago. Now it was just dirt and weeds enclosed by a low fence. Or maybe it had been some kind of pen, for pigs, sheep, or rabbits. The enclosure bordered right on the house, and from the two windows on that side hung air conditioners going full blast. Daddy was working.

Inside, the cottage had a nice glow in the daylight, and it was just beginning to grow warm in the late morning. Upstairs, the lace curtains stirred while I changed from my damp running clothes to clean shorts and a T-shirt. I was careful not to mess my hair. It was smooth and pulled tight from my face. I peered at myself in the small mirror. She had made me look rich. Almost. I dabbed some blush on my cheeks. Slipped my small gold hoops into my ears. *Now* I looked rich. I brushed my eyebrows up into little feathers, like Simone's.

"Ali? Ali? You back?" Daddy was standing at the foot of the loft ladder. I looked down at him. I was barefoot, in shorts and a T-shirt, a faint mist of sweat already gathering on my lip, and there he was in corduroy pants, with a woolen shirt over his turtleneck. I couldn't help laughing.

"You look funny," I told him, starting down the ladder.

"Look funny. Work good," he said.

"You'd never be a Hemingway, Daddy, out on the African plains, sweating over a typewriter."

"You're right. But who wants to be Hemingway? Want to join me for a cup of coffee? My machine's busy printing out a chapter at the moment."

I could hear the printer pounding away. "Where?" I asked. "I'm not going in there to freeze. Are you going to sit out here and melt?"

He began slipping the woolen shirt off. "I'll adapt," he said. "Anything for a little company."

"And a cup of coffee," I teased.

He put his arm around my shoulder. His hands were wintery.

In the kitchen I filled the teapot with water and put it on to boil. I counted out scoops of coffee into the lined funnel. "If it's companionship you want, I hear Mrs. Silver is just dying to have you over for a dinner party."

"Oy."

"Not only that, but she's stocking up her liquor cabinet."

"Well, I hope you told them how unsocial I am when I'm in the middle of writing a book."

"Of course. I told them you never socialize, and I told them you've been in AA for fifteen years, and she'd just have to drink it all herself."

He looked amused. "You did?"

"Daddy! Of course not. I just said you were busy on a book and not going out. That's all." I sat across the table from him and put my chin in my palm and stared at him. "And guess what."

"What?"

"Guess what Simone's mother has growing in her garden."

"Can't imagine."

"Grass."

Daddy stared at me. "Grass?"

"You know, *grass* grass. Pot. Reefer leaves. Marijuana."

"In her garden?"

"Right out in the open."

"Hunh."

"Is that all you can say—hunh? Isn't that illegal? Shouldn't someone report her?"

"I don't know. I don't like to get involved with judging people and pointing fingers. Besides, why report her? She's only hurting herself."

"And everyone around her," I said.

"Ali. Sometimes you sound awfully self-righteous."

I straightened and leaned back into the chair. Maybe he was right. I wasn't sure. It was none of my business, except I was real curious to meet her. "Wish you'd go there."

"Ali," he moaned, and that was his answer. I knew how he hated to see anyone but his AA cronies when he was writing. "Are you bored?" he asked.

"No! I'm not bored. I told you I wouldn't be bored. And even if I was, I wouldn't admit it."

"How about coming to an open meeting with me tonight? There's one in Harborville, across the ferry. Why don't you come? It's been a long time."

The water began to whistle. The long day stretched out ahead of me. Why not? That would give me something to do tonight. "Okay," I told him. I poured the water over the coffee grounds, and some of it splashed out onto the stove. I wiped it up, wishing we had a Ramona to make us coffee and serve us out in the garden. I thought of Daddy and me sitting out in the enclosed garden, maybe a pig or two snorting at our feet. I laughed out loud, startling Daddy.

"What's so funny?" he asked.

"Oh, nothing. I was just thinking about us being rich. How it would be."

"That's funny?" he asked.

"The way we'd do it, it would be," I said. I glanced at him there at the table. He was starting to look warm and uncomfortable. "Coffee's almost done," I said. "Don't worry. I'll have a cup ready for you before that ice melts off your mustache."

Simone

The beach is exactly as I remembered it. At home the neighborhood changes all the time—new buildings going up, stores changing from delis to florists, new faces on doormen, different people rushing by, but here, here on Dune Island, time has slowed to a stop. It is exactly as it was when I was a young child. I slip off my sandals, leaving them on the grass, and walk down to the water's edge. The sand is full of shells and I walk lightly. I am not used to them yet. I feel like Mother is watching from the house. She probably isn't but it's an old feeling, and unlike other days when I would pretend she was watching and dance up and down the beach, today I imagine I feel her eyes on me and I turn my back to the house, move away from it. The beach is uniform for miles, the same shells, the same view, but I will walk down a mile or two to get away from her eyes.

Two estates down, our neighbors' dock has collapsed in the middle. This is the only change here. There was an early spring hurricane that cracked it in half as if it were made of matchsticks. I look at the house up on the hilly shore. Its shutters are still locked over the windows. No one is here yet. When they come there will be a boat. Maybe they will tie up at our dock and workmen will come and rebuild theirs.

I think of the time Father decided to strengthen the pilings on our dock. Three men had come, jovial, slow-moving island men. That day Mother brought them beer, and I went with her. I remember her sitting there perched on the edge of the pier, her long almost-skinny legs swinging in the summer air, and I'd been pleased to be with her while she was so happy. In front of them, she startled me by drawing me next to her and running her fingers through my hair. She told them how pretty I'd be one day, and they had said—like her mother, one day she'll be just like her mother.

Even then I had quickly taken stock, in a panic to reassure myself. No, I was not like her at all. Our hands were different, hers thin and birdlike, mine fleshier with rounder fingernails, her feet narrow, mine wide with a high arch, my nose clearly my father's and not hers, and unlike her, I had not liked the beer they passed around that afternoon. Holding my lips to the can—just a sip, Mother said—I did not like getting past the suds to get to the taste, and once there, the bitter, bubbly taste held no charms for me. But I stayed, a willing prisoner in my mother's infrequent touch, and I had watched the men pose with their shovels, flirt with my mother, and then when the beer cans were empty they had heaved the creosote-darkened posts with their muscles bulging.

Mother led the way back to the house, smiling. I knew somehow not to mention the men to Father. When he asked of the progress on the dock, she spoke of the thickness of the new pilings, the time the island men arrived, but neither of us mentioned the laughter, her arms around me, or the shared beer. Me because I was a little afraid. Mother because . . . because, well, I think she had forgotten.

The water laps around my feet. It is cold, but if I walk a ways into the water, my feet touch sand, not shells, and it's a little kinder on my winter soles. When I have gone far enough, when I am just a speck from any window back at the house, I walk up the beach, unflinching, willing my feet to toughen up now, and then when I am at the high-tide line, where the shells have accumulated the thickness of buttons in a barrel, I do what I have always done, every summer since Adilia. I collect jingle shells for my promise bracelet.

Ali

I wasn't used to the ferry yet, so just like the tourists, as soon as the car was parked I hopped out and went to stand by the railing. Daddy'd been on the island awhile, ferrying back and forth to meetings, but he came, too, and smiled out over the water. He breathed deep, and I felt his contentment now that he was away from his work and satisfied. The ferry pulled away from Dune Island and drew slowly toward the distant shore. It wasn't far. A bridge would've done nicely, but the islanders loved their privacy and were arrogant enough to make it difficult to get to them. Like a moat around a castle, the waters protected them from too much tourism, too many summer people.

"Haven't gotten ahold of your book yet," the ferryman said to Daddy, punching his ticket. "I looked for it, but the library still doesn't have it. And I looked in the supermarket at the books they have there, and I didn't see it."

"No kidding," Daddy said. "Maybe you've got to ask the librarian to get it. She probably would, you know."

"Naw, old Gertrude doesn't want any newfangled books

crowdin' up her shelves. Only classics and best-sellers, she says. That's what people read. But I'd read yours if I could get it." He handed the ticket back to Daddy, nodded, and moved on.

"Good grief," I said. "Why don't you just give him a copy?"

"We have this same conversation every time I see him," Daddy whispered to me. "If I gave him the book, we'd have nothing to talk about." He laughed and leaned on the railing. I leaned next to him, arm to arm, almost shoulder to shoulder, and we watched Harborville come closer and closer.

Most Alcoholics Anonymous meetings are in church basements, and seeing as how I've been going to them most of my life, I ought to know. I get touchy sometimes about AA and my father being a recovering alcoholic. The couple of times it's come up with friends who found out, I didn't like it. They think alcoholics are derelicts, or else sober misfits walking around with white knuckles, flying like madmen away from whiskey bottles. They know Daddy, like him, and then when they find out he's an alcoholic, they want to know if he gets drunk sometimes, as if they'd found out he's a vampire and they want to know if he goes out every night. Does he grow fangs? Do I keep a silver spike in my drawer? It's crazy. So I don't like to talk about it, but once in a while, I love to go to an open meeting with Daddy. It's outrageous to walk into a church basement with him and get this indescribable sense of how loved he is, and not because he's a writer, some kind of celebrity—most of them probably don't even know—but just because he's Charlie M., sober, an old-timer, and this month's coffee-maker.

We were the first ones there that night, and I helped Daddy lug the coffee pots from the back closet. I rolled out the white-paper tablecloths on the long tables, smoothing them and crimping the edges so they'd stay down. I had to smile. When I was little I'd go to this one meeting with Daddy and bring my marking pens. I wasn't really interested in what was being said, but I'd spend the whole time drawing colorful scenes on the table, and at this meeting they had kept the tablecloth for a while, and whenever I came back it would be tacked on the wall next to the Steps and Traditions.

Some people started drifting in and the kitchen was soon a hub of laughter and conversation. I felt a little nervous. I didn't know anyone there yet, so I kept busy. I put up the little table signs, *Easy Does It*; *Keep It Simple, Stupid*, and tossed a basket on each table. A couple of people smiled at me and I smiled back. I liked pretending I was an alcoholic. I knew that's what they thought at first, seeing me there, setting up, but soon Daddy called and started introducing me around.

When the meeting started, I settled down into my wooden folding chair beside Daddy and kind of went into a trance. I half listened. I knew the preamble like some people know prayers or the Pledge of Allegiance. "Alcoholics Anonymous is a fellowship of men and women . . . the only requirement for membership is a desire to stop drinking . . . there are no dues or fees . . . and to help other alcoholics to achieve sobriety." I knew it by heart.

The meeting went on. The first speaker was introduced, a dapper old guy with a yellow tie and kelly-green sports jacket, and as slowly and as surely as the tide comes in, as he filled our minds with stories of his ragged past, the room began to fill with pale, curling cigarette smoke. Strange, but I loved it. I looked around at the people: a rich-looking woman smartly dressed beside a poor man in a too-heavy sweater; a serious-looking pipe smoker next to a woman whose eyes were red and scared; three old men along the wall, kind of pompous like concrete statues; and at one table I noticed a young man. He was listening intently to the speaker. Daddy always said how he liked to see young people come in. That they didn't have to wait till they'd lost everything before they came to AA.

I watched him, wondered about him, and then he picked up his Styrofoam cup and sipped his coffee. His attention left the speaker and he looked around the room. His eyes met mine for the briefest instant without any recognition and then he turned back to the speaker. But I had recognized him. I stared at him, at his dark skin, his thick mustache. He was the water-skier from that morning. The one Simone had liked.

I could barely wait for the coffee break. I knew I could say hello to him here. Everyone spoke to everyone else easily, without knowing names or anything. I'd seen motorcycle guys talking to old ladies, stuffy-looking matrons laughing with women who looked like they came from the bad end of the night. I just knew I'd have no problem. And wouldn't Simone be surprised? The next day at the Pridley beach, I could introduce her to him, before she'd even get a chance to do her thing and get into action. She would die.

I thought the old guy with the yellow tie would never get to the part where he found AA and his life changed for the better. Daddy even glanced at me at one point. I must have been squirming out of my skin. Finally, finally, he was done and they called a coffee break. I was the first one at the coffee machine, half filling my cup with dark hot coffee and topping it off with milk. I waited at the counter stirring forever. Everyone said hello. Even Daddy, who introduced me to more friends. My eyes kept flitting down the line. The mustache was getting closer. When at last he was right there, filling his own Styrofoam cup, I said, "Hi."

He looked at me and smiled, but didn't say anything.

"Wasn't that you this morning hanging off the back of the Pridley motorboat?" I asked. I sipped my warm coffee and studied him over the rim. He was older than I had thought. There was gray in his hair above his ears, and even in his mustache a little, but his eyes looked like they were a hundred years old, something sad and tired about them.

He squinted at me. "Yeah, I guess that was me. Did I see you?" He was inching away, leaving his coffee black.

I was kind of relieved he didn't recognize me. After all, it had been from a distance, and I'd been drippy sweaty and red as a beet. "I was with my friend on the little pier," I tried.

He looked puzzled. "The little pier?"

Jeez, where was it? "On Dune Island. I don't know where exactly. We were out running, and we stopped there and you rode by."

"Oh!" Suddenly he stopped inching away. "The two girls on the pier!"

Amazing! Brilliant deduction. How long had he been sober? Maybe he was still clearing up.

"Of course! Small world," he added, suddenly warm and happy, as if he remembered me from his childhood. "Well, what brings you here? How long've you been in?"

"Actually, I'm not *in*. I'm Charlie's daughter. Just here for an open meeting. Daddy thinks that a family that goes to meetings together stays together."

"Charlie? Charlie?" He was trying to put us together.

I pointed to my father, who was standing by the doorway with some other men.

"Oh, Charlie. Right. I know him. A lot of time, right?"

"Fifteen years sober," I said.

"Whew. Can't imagine it. I've got my ninety days and I'm amazed."

I didn't know what to say.

"So!" He didn't know what to say either. "You going to be back at the pier tomorrow morning again, to supply us with another audience?"

"Actually my friend, Simone, was talking about going to the Pridley beach for a swim."

"Simone?"

"Simone Silver. She lives next door to where we're staying."

He seemed surprised. "Simone Silver? The princess of Dune Island?"

My mouth dropped open and I stood gaping at him. "You know her?"

"Of her. Of her," he corrected. "Everyone knows of her and her family, especially her mother's parties. They're notorious on the island. Can't say I ever made one myself. Not that I wouldn't have loved it. But that's all over for me now." He looked sad.

"Why?"

"Lion's den," he answered. And then as if by rote: "If you're not a lion tamer, don't go into the lion's den. My drinking and drugging days are over.

"Well, listen, it was nice meeting you." He held out his hand to shake mine, typical AA fashion. "I'm Frank. Make sure you see me tomorrow at the Pridley. I'll get you some rafts. If you want I'll even get you both a paddle boat. And introduce you to the guys." He began drifting back to his seat, leaving me standing there.

"Frank," I called after him.

He turned and looked at me.

"Don't mention where you met me."

He laughed. "Don't *you* mention where you met *me!*"

"Just say you're a friend of my father's, okay?"

"Gotcha," he said. He turned and walked away.

Someone was pounding the gavel to introduce the next speaker. I slid into my seat. It would be nice to already know someone at the Pridley tomorrow. Someone to "introduce us to the guys." Simone would be impressed, that's for sure. I could never tell her what Frank had said though, about her mother's parties being a lion's den. But with my connections I'd be able to get Simone Silver, princess of Dune Island, a paddle boat. At your service, your highness.

Simone

Larsen has wiped down the bicycles for us. I give Ali the newer one. It is brighter, shinier, but mine is lighter. I wait for her at the top of the last hill. The pine trees stand so quiet around us. Not even a breeze from the bay. And the sun is hard and bare. A good day for a tan.

Ali is bent over almost in half, trudging my new bike up the hill. "Jeez, I don't know how you do it," she says, coming up even with me and pressing the back of her hand across her damp upper lip.

"You have to build up speed on the downhill part," I tell her. "Then just put it in low gear and pedal steady."

She gets this sarcastic thing that kind of twitches over her face and disappears into her voice. "No kidding. You mean I'm not supposed to keep the brakes on?"

"Come on," I say, getting back on my bike. "That was the biggest hill. The rest is cake."

"I don't want to sound like a five-year-old or anything, but are we almost there yet, Mommy, are we almost there?"

"Another mile," I tell her over my shoulder, riding off, "and it's all downhill."

"Oh, great," I hear her mutter as she gets back up on her seat. "I can't wait to come back this way, a whole mile uphill for starters. What do you do for fun, Princess? Roll trucks? Plow fields?"

She's ridiculous. Maybe the summer would be easier without her. I feel a hundred years older than she is, like I'm her mother almost. I can't believe her nails. Or that she stuck her hair in pigtails. Pigtails! But she's company, I guess. Somebody to do things with, to run off with. Especially being Charles A. Mintz's daughter. That's carte blanche for me this summer with Mother—like this morning. Where will you be? With Ali. Where are you going? With Ali. When will you be back? When Ali comes back. I would live alone if I could. No questions, no parents. And then I wouldn't need friends either. I could be a mysterious young woman living alone in the penthouse of an exclusive building, maybe by the river. Maybe have a modeling career, or design clothes, or be the president of a multibillion-dollar cosmetic line. I'd ride a Rolls with a chauffeur. Wear a floor-length sable coat over my leotards to go to my exercise class. Diamonds. I'd go to the islands every winter, Paris in the spring—

"Hey! Earth calling her highness!" Ali pulls up next to me, yelling.

"What?"

"Where are you? Did you lose your hearing in your

skiing accident, too, or are you trying to levitate or something?"

"Just thinking," I tell her, the jewels and exotic places vanishing into thin air.

"I have a surprise for you," she says. She's smiling now, pedaling along.

"What is it?" I wonder what ridiculous thing it is she thinks will surprise me. Has she brought peanut-butter sandwiches in her lunch basket? Yoo-Hoos?

"I can't tell you yet. But you're going to find out real soon. Soon as we get to the Pridley beach."

The suspense is killing me. I yawn.

And then the road widens ahead, banks and tilts down to the beach. Out of the woods of oak and pine opens a wide expansive view of the harbor, blue and sparkling, and today there are multicolored sailboats like small paper origami birds fluttering over its surface.

"Oh, how beautiful!" she cries, and flies past me downhill, no hands, her arms flung into the air.

"Downhill champ," I say to myself. Listen to me. I'm beginning to sound just like her.

The Pridley sits up on a hill behind the road, its wide drives leading down to the road and across the road to its narrow beach on the bay. It's noon and there are people on the sand in wooden beach chairs and under colored umbrellas. We lock our bikes on the awning pier, unload our towels and food baskets from the backs of the bikes, and I start to head down onto the sand. But Ali is smiling and searching, as if she's looking for someone she knows. And then she's waving, grinning at a man on the pier. "Frank!" she calls. "Frank!"

He lifts his head from the ropes of one of Pridley's rowboats and turns. I recognize him right away, and can't believe her. "Ali!" I whisper. "That's the water-skier from yesterday."

She gives me a quick casual glance as she throws her towel over her shoulder and starts over to him. "I know. It's my old friend Frank."

I'm following her. Her old friend Frank?

"Hi, there," this Frank says. "So you made it out here after all. You drive?"

"Nah," she tells him. "We biked. Getting our exercise for the day."

"Biked?" he asks. "Over those hills?"

"Piece of cake," she tells him. She doesn't even look at me. "Frank, this is my friend Simone. Simone, Frank." Funny, but he shakes my hand. He's older than I thought. But handsome. I can tell he knows he's handsome, something in his eyes and the way he looks at me.

"Nice to meet you, Simone." He turns to Ali. "I don't think you told me your name last night," he says.

Old friend?

She frowns. "Ali."

"So what are you girls going to do today?" he asks. "Catch some rays?"

"Yeah. Maybe swim a little," Ali answers. "Borrow a

couple of rubber rafts. Can you get us a paddle boat later?"

"For you, Ali, anything. As a matter of fact—" He looks around for somebody. "Maybe Brendan and Sammy could take you out water-skiing later if they have some free time."

"Oh! I don't believe it! That would be great! Wouldn't it, Simone?"

It terrifies me. The water. Standing on water way out in the middle of the bay. Being pulled, jerked by a motorboat. But Brendan and Sammy. "I don't know," I say. "I've never water-skied."

"It's easy," he tells me. "Just like skiing in the snow, only it's wet and you get a tow."

"I've never skied in the snow either," I laugh, and the minute it's out of my mouth, I know I've made a terrible mistake.

Ali is staring at me. "Of course you have," she says quietly.

"I don't swim very well, is what I mean." An old feeling creeps over me, a nauseousness in my soul. My lies are like grapes. I pop them in my mouth over and over, easily and without effort, and once in a while one turns bad, slimy and powdery on my tongue. I don't look at Ali.

"Well, tell you what," Frank says. "Grab a couple of rubber rafts down there if you want. Tell the kid I said so. And catch some rays. Float around. And later I'll either get you a paddle boat or the motorboat. Whichever you decide."

"Sounds good," Ali answers him. Her voice sounds soft and distant to me. I know she is thinking other things as she speaks to him. I feel all frozen inside, frozen, knowing I must either attack or run. Our bikes are locked together. She has the key. "See you later, then," she says, and leads the way back down the pier to the sand. Frank turns back to his work, and I follow her.

There is a part up the middle of Ali's head that separates her two ridiculous pigtails. My mind is scrambling for something to say. The part is perfectly straight and self-righteous. There are a few freckles on the back of her neck. I must be the first to speak. "Old friend," I snicker under my breath, but loud enough for her to hear.

She stops dead in her tracks right in front of a family laid out in the sand, and I almost run into her. "What did you say?"

"I said some old friend he is," passing her and walking on to a clear spot of beach. "At first I couldn't imagine why you wouldn't have said something yesterday when we first saw him if he was such a great old friend, and then he doesn't even know your name." I smile and gaze out onto the bay, lifting my hair from my shoulders, twisting and knotting it on top of my head. She drops her towel and stares at me.

"So I exaggerated a little. I met him last night. He's an old friend of my *father's*." She's defensive and tense. I spread out my thick towel and center my shadow exactly over it. I slip out of my shorts and T-shirt, down to my bathing suit. "But what's *your* excuse, your highness? What was that bit about the skiing accident you ran by me yesterday?"

"Oh, Ali, stop it. It was just a harmless joke. You should have seen your face. Doctors said I'd never walk again, and there I was jogging with you." I am laughing now, settling into the sand on my back, my eyes closed, the sun already warming me. "Don't make such a big deal. We're even, right?" I lift my head, and shading my eyes with my hand, I check her stony face. "I got one on you, you got one on me."

She is blocking the sun and all I can see is her dark shape above me, hands on hips, fingers tapping. "I didn't know this was a lie meet. What will we do? At the end of the summer, whoever's the biggest bullshit artist will get the prize?"

"If you want." I wish she'd move and let the sun shine on me.

"Fine." I hear her spreading her towel next to me, muttering.

The sun is warming my face like a thick glove. My very breath seems to be pulled out of me and released. There's a clunk of soda cans, a tossing of clothes, a small spray of sand. "I'll be back," she says, and I don't even open my eyes. "I'm going to swim out to the raft," she says very deliberately, "and send up smoke signals for Mick Jagger. Where are my matches? He's staying at a room up at the Pridley. I told him I'd let him know when I arrived, and you know Mick, he's always so prompt. . . ."

It goes on and on and finally her voice and her splashing disappear into the distance and a little coil in me unwinds, softens. I don't know why I had said that yesterday about a skiing accident. I wish I hadn't. I lift my head in time to see her hoist herself up on the raft out in the bay. Her two pigtails hang like snakes from her ears. From a distance I kind of like them. I smile, but there's that old, deep familiar ache in my throat.

Ali

I was out of there, mentally, emotionally, and physically, as far away as I could get on the raft. Somehow our two bikes chained together locked us with each other for the day. I didn't want to leave the beach; I wanted to be there. Actually, if she had left it would have been ideal, but there she was, rolling like a bird on a rotisserie, and I'm sure she was as determined as I was to stay as long as she pleased. I resigned myself to a day of dark silence. At least I'd get a tan.

I sat out on the wooden raft as long as I could, cooling off, trying to get a little perspective on things. *How important is it?* Daddy would have said. Yeah, what's the big deal, so the girl lies like a rug. I sat there on the edge of the raft until the toasted edges of my body began to tell me that if I didn't get back to the towel soon I would have a burn on my shoulders, the fronts of my thighs, and the top of my head. Period. I slid off into the water and headed back to my towel.

She didn't even open her eyes. She could have been asleep. I rubbed lotion all over myself where I could reach, noticing how on me it soaked right in, but on Simone her lotion made her glisten like a tropical fish. I dug my book out of my bag and tried to read. Next to me, Simone rolled onto her back and I ignored her.

"Come on, girls, let's move it a little. You're going to fry, seize up if you don't get your exercise today." It was Frank, standing there at the edge of our towels with a big orange inflatable raft under each arm. But best of all, best of all, he was flanked by Brendan and Sammy.

I rolled over and looked up at them. They were standing there, grinning and cocky. And if I had thought yesterday that the guy driving the boat had looked good from a distance, I was in for a surprise on closer inspection. He was gorgeous.

Frank introduced them. "Brendan," he said, nudging him, and "Sammy," he said, nudging the other guy, who was kind of ordinary, but I hardly noticed him, I was having such a hard time keeping my eyes off Brendan. "These two lovely ladies are Simone"—she perched her sunglasses on top of her head and smiled slightly—"and Ali."

"Hi."

"How's it goin'?"

"Hi."

Oh, God, how I hated stuff like that. Introductions, manners, beginnings. I wanted Brendan to know me already for a million years, so I wouldn't have to feel so shaky and uncertain. I wanted him to know what a great person I was under this roundish body. I wanted Simone to blow away into the sand like a washed-over sand castle. I remember thinking, Now hold on, Ali, maybe he likes middle class, ordinary. Maybe he really appreciates that not-so-perfect look, that dynamic smile with slightly crooked teeth. He would see the true value here, go with the good stuff, see through Simone's facade instantly. Or would he want perfect? Teeth, skin, figure, even if she was conceited and probably a chronic liar. All this ran through my head in a fraction of a second, in the breath it takes to say hi-how's-it-going-hi, as I lay there in the sun, half-naked next to Miss Perfect.

Frank dumped the two rafts at our feet. "It's a great day for white-water rafting," he said. Behind him tiny waves lapped weakly on the sand. "Or shark baiting. Whatever. These guys have to mend some sails today, but I told them you'd like to go water-skiing one day."

"You two aren't registered here at the hotel, are you?" Sammy asked. He had eyes like my father's dog, soft and patient.

"No," Simone answered, a certain music to her voice that I'd never heard before. "We live on Shell Beach on the West Neck."

"You sisters or something?" Brendan asked.

"Hardly," I answered, no music to this old voice. "Just neighbors."

"Well, listen," Sammy said, "if you want to go skiing, just let us know a day or two ahead of time, so we can make sure we get you two in the schedule. Hotel people first, but"—he shrugged—"nobody keeps track."

"Yeah," Brendan said, his eyes flashing at me and then Simone, but me first, I noticed. "Just give us a day or two notice."

"Thanks a lot," I said. "It looked like a lot of fun when we saw you yesterday."

Brendan smiled. "Frank said that was you two."

"Yeah, it was." I was grinning. Jeez, I hated myself. I sounded like a Brenda Starr comic strip.

Someone whistled from the dock. Sammy whistled back, with two fingers to his mouth, not far from Brendan's ear. Brendan rolled his eyes and I heard myself giggle as if I were about twelve.

"Gotta go," Sammy said, with a little salute to us and a punch to Brendan's arm. "Sails are ready. Catch you two later."

"Maybe," Simone answered. What a great answer. It actually made Brendan hesitate and look at her. Then smiles, waves, nods, a splash of sand on our towels, and they were gone. We watched them walk away, straight strong legs, broad backs, and Brendan so golden and electric. I felt as if a tidal wave had just hit us and now slid back into the bay. Simone and I looked at each other.

"Whew," I said, all else forgotten between us for the moment. "Is he beautiful or what?"

"He likes you," she said, sitting up.

"Likes me? What are you talking about? Get out of here!"

"No, I can tell about stuff like that. Don't you think I could tell you like him?"

"Oh, no, I hope not."

"Don't be silly. It's the most natural thing in the world, and it was written all over both your faces. It's attraction, like magnets. All your little metal filings were waving in the air, yelling, Me! Me! Me!"

"Get lost!" but I laughed. Was she right? Could she tell already that he was interested in me? In me? With Simone Silver, princess of Dune Island right beside me? I doubted it, strongly doubted it, but I wanted to believe every word she ever said.

"Ali Mintz," she said, looking at me now and smiling her charm-school smile like you could die, "you are about to have the summer of your life. I think this is it."

Simone

The shower water is so hot, and my skin so tender from the sun, that it feels like sparklers all over my body. Already I have a ruby glow that will make me as dark as an Indian by the end of the summer. The backs of my hands are a different shade, and my fingernails are like pale shells. The bathroom window looks out through ferns to the dark bay, but I don't hide my nakedness. I am a squaw, stepping out from beneath a waterfall. I wrap the towel loosely around me and go out to lie on my bed. I think about nothing. About everything. My mind feels like the ocean at that point where it changes from high tide to low tide, that instant where all energy is lost and pressures ease.

My pillow slides to the floor, leaving Adilia's tarot cards, wrapped in silk. Maybe it's time. Reaching for them, I unwind the scarf and sit up, the towel dropping from me. The cards are heavy and thick as I shuffle them, bigger than playing cards, making my hands feel like a child's. How large her hands had seemed, how strong, and how deep her voice had been, deep and sure and penetrating like notes from a cello—"Today, yesterday, tomorrow, ago, and to be," she would chant, spreading out the five cards as I do now.

As soon as they are down, I remember that I haven't asked a question, and yet all five cards are upside down, not good. I shuffle again, over and over, trying to come up with a question.

Suddenly my door opens and Mother is standing there. "Simone?" Our eyes meet and immediately she looks away and puts her hand to her eyes as if to shade them. "For God's sake, Simone, get dressed. How can you sit around that way? You'll catch your death."

"Mother, if you'd knock you'd save yourself a lot of trauma." I continue shuffling and stare at her.

"Really, Simone. This is not a nudist colony. Despite what you think. What would you do if your father came in?"

"Father knocks," I say, and then, taunting her, "Come. Come in, Mother, and cut the cards. Ask a question. I'll tell you your fortune."

She has forgotten my nakedness and stares at the cards. "I thought you'd gotten rid of those things," she says, "those voodoo cards. Didn't you learn a lesson from that woman and what all her mumbo jumbo did for her?"

"Is that your question, Mother?" I feel myself get hard like gravel. Loudly I say, "Did Simone learn a lesson from *that woman* and all her mumbo jumbo?" I deal out the cards in turn. "Today, yesterday, tomorrow, ago, and to be." The cards are all up. "The answer is yes! Simone *did* learn a lesson." I am suddenly quiet. Adilia's card has actually turned up before me—the dark-haired Queen of Swords, the poor queen. My skin suddenly feels cold, and now I am sorry for my nakedness. It is in the "ago" spot, and I feel as if Adilia has just drawn her hand across my shoulders. I pull the towel up around me and grow quiet.

"Stop it, Simone. I just wanted to know if you are coming down anymore. Or are you up for the night?"

"Why?" I ask. She looks small in the doorway, like a waif, an orphan. Too skinny. My own mother. I feel like I see her through a peep hole in a fence. She's so far away.

"I just wanted to know," she says. She doesn't look at me, even though I have pulled the towel up over my breasts. "I want to, um, turn out the lights, you know, if you're not going back down anymore."

Why is she nervous? Is she getting ready to drink? "Where's Father?"

"He's staying in the city tonight. He would've gotten out here too late to catch the ferry. He'll be out tomorrow, though, and then maybe we can take the Jag and go to the city and go shopping. Would you like that?"

"No." I pick up the cards and begin reshuffling. "Has Ramona gone?"

"Yes, of course."

"Are you going to bed now?" Her arms are at her sides, her hands are empty. No glass sloshing.

"As soon as I turn out the lights and lock up," she says.

"I'll turn out the lights," I say, testing her. "As soon as I get dressed."

"No, no, no," she says, cooperative and insistent. "No bother. Really. I'll just lock up, and I'll be out like a light tonight. I can feel it. I'm sleepy." She fakes a yawn and I watch her, my mother who is never sleepy, who finds sleep only in a scotch bottle. I feel as if my antenna has unfurled, like on Father's Jag, a buzz and it appears, listening to the air.

"So you just stay right where you are, darling, naked as a blue jay if that's what makes you happy, and I'll take care of things. Sleep tight now." She backs out of the doorway and closes it with a snap. I have a feeling she'd lock it if she could.

I'm all uneasy. Something's not right in a way that's too familiar. The room tilts and I look back at the cards. "What's wrong with my mother?" I ask, laying out the five cards. I forget I can ask only yes-no questions. And two are up and three are upside down. I scoop them up and shuffle. "Should I go downstairs and see what's happening?" Today, yesterday, tomorrow, ago, and to be. Four upside down, one up. A clear no. But my room tips again and I slide off my bed, pull on my long T-shirt, and shut my light. I hear a car pull up outside. I hope it's

Father and go to the window. But I don't recognize the car. An old scratched-up convertible. I feel the front door open and close downstairs in the soles of my feet. And then the car pulls away. When it gets to the end of the driveway, its radio blasts out and it drives away past the trees. Who was that? Has mother left?

I press my ear to the door and listen. There's movement downstairs in the front parlor. I hear the French doors to the porch close, the piano lid close, and the clock bongs six times, all off and too slow. I wait for Mother to fix it, to hear the winding of the clock, the extra bongs, but it grows very quiet. I open my door and step out into the hall. The only light is from downstairs, and it casts a shadow through the banister, like welts across my legs. I start down the steps. Not a sound. I stop and listen. She's walking around the room and I hear her collapse onto the sofa by the window and sigh. I listen for ice cubes and continue down, my bare feet sinking into the thick carpet. Without a sound I walk across the hall and press myself against the wall by the entrance way to the parlor. She is doing something. I hear paper tear, and something drop onto the glass table. She is very still.

I draw closer to the doorway and look. I see my mother. She is sitting on the sofa, leaning over the table, and she is carefully pouring some white powder on the glass. I almost smile at the craziness of it—is my mother about to make a wish? Did Adilia once pile hollyhock pollen for my mother and instruct her in wish making? But Mother doesn't make a wish. She shapes the powder into two long, thin lines, holds a straw to her mouth, no, her nose, takes a deep breath, the loudest noise she has made, and the powder disappears up into her nose. The second line disappears as well.

I step into the open doorway and shout at her. "Mother! What are you doing?"

She looks up at me, startled, slips something into her pocket, but stays there, waiting for something she expects. Waiting, as if I'll disappear if she waits another minute more. "Simone," she says stupidly, "you're up." A trace of powder dusts her lip. In two strides I am in front of her, tearing the paper on the table, grabbing the straw from her hand, and I would wipe the powder from her lip, but I don't dare touch her. I would kill her.

"Are you doing drugs now too?" I shout. "Don't you know how bad this is for you? It'll destroy you."

"It will? You think so?" Her eyes are black and huge, and a warm flush spreads over her face and neck. "Oh, Simone, everything's so dramatic for you. It's just a little blow—don't make such a big deal. And what are you doing up? You said you'd be going right to sleep."

"And you said you were locking up. Locking up, all right. Locking up your brain."

"Simone. Simone. It's a powdered highball, that's all. Only it's better than a highball. I can handle it. I don't pass out, I don't forget the next morning. It's my answer."

"Mother, don't."

"Don't what?"

"Please don't use that stuff. Please." I feel so weak, so powerless. I have to make her promise. I even sit next to her, and now I reach out and brush the stuff off her lip. I wipe my fingers on my shirt.

"Simone—"

"No, Mother. Just promise me, please."

She is silent.

"I'll do anything."

She's smiling now. I want it to be my closeness, my caring, that makes her smile like that, but I think it's the cocaine. She reaches out and touches my cheek. "Why don't we go shopping tomorrow, darling? Wouldn't that be nice? A couple of days in the city together. Just the two of us?"

Maybe if I get her away from here for a while. Maybe if I spend some time with her, she will be different. I nod.

"Good!" She bounds out of her seat. She looks so happy, so energetic. Maybe she's right. Maybe it is different from the drinks. "Listen, I'm going to go for a hike on the beach. Want to come?" She presses her fists deep in her pockets and backs off before I can answer. "On second thought," she says, "I think you should rest. We have a big day tomorrow."

Before I can say a word, she has scooped a sweater up off the piano bench and bounced out of the room, leaving me there alone. I hear the back door close. I hear her singing.

Slowly, deliberately, I clean up the mess she has left behind. I crush the paper and the straw in my hand, and then, leaning over the glass table, I wipe it over and over again with the hem of my T-shirt until nothing is left. Nothing is left.

Ali

I used to wonder what it would be like to have someone in love with me. Really in love with me. I had some vague ideas about it, you know, like maybe he'd do something like paint my name on an overpass on the East Island Expressway. I'd be driving along the Expressway in the little sports car I knew I'd have someday, and there it would be, for the whole world to see, written in bold graffiti letters across an overpass: I LOVE YOU, ALI. I had seen it many times, with many names, but never mine. I'd always imagined the guy doing it. Pictured him bending over the railing with a spray can, maybe even tied to the railing so he wouldn't fall off. But of course there was no expressway on Dune Island. There weren't even any traffic lights. So I wasn't sure what form love could take out there.

These were the important kinds of things I was coming up with that summer on my long walks along the beach with Lois. I tossed sticks of driftwood over the dunes for her to bring back to me. Daddy said this summer was a good opportunity for her to get the exercise she didn't normally get. But that was another thing I thought about. *Was* it good? Wouldn't she go home now in the fall to our brownstone and feel hemmed in, long for the unending stretches of beach? Wouldn't it be better if she had never known about long romps and open spaces? Kind of like me . . . Wouldn't I have been better off if I'd never met Simone, with her pool and her servants? Weren't there some things in my life that I wished I'd never seen or known?

I hated these walks. I thought too much. But I loved them, too. That was the problem. Everything in my life had "no" part and a "yes" part. I could see all sides sometimes, the positives and the negatives, till everything and nothing made sense.

I kept thinking about Simone. She had just sort of disappeared. Not that I went looking for her or anything, but I thought she'd be around, wanting to go to the beach again, or go catch Brendan and Sammy. But she hadn't come by for a couple of days, and I wasn't about to go calling for her myself.

Remembering Simone made me think of running or jogging again. Or maybe biking. She had told me to keep her extra bike at the cottage and use it for the summer. I thought of biking back to the Pridley. Looking for Brendan. Saying hello to Frank. As soon as I thought of it, I headed back to the cottage. Lois was reluctant to follow. I threw the driftwood ahead and she would get it and run back in the other direction, almost as if she were pleading with me to stay. But I plodded on, over the hard sand, up through the cutting shells and over the dunes and grasses, back to the cottage. She followed far behind.

The windows to father's study were frosting around the air conditioners, and when I went inside he was sitting at the table in the kitchen. "You missed your mother. She just called," he said, looking up at me, his reading glasses perched on his head. "She wanted to know if you were bored yet. Are you?"

I sat opposite him. "Do you know there's frost on your windows?"

"I asked first," he said. "Are you bored?"

"How can I be bored in a summer house where there's frost on the windows?"

"Well, she's worried that you're sitting around staring at a television, eating potato chips, and driving me crazy. She's coming out to see for herself."

"We don't have a television."

"She's sure you smuggled one in."

"Well, did you tell her I've already read four books and worked all the fat off Lois?"

"I told her you met the Silvers' daughter, and you've been running and biking and swimming."

"Sounds good to me," I answered. "So what's her problem?"

"No problem. She wants to see for herself, so she can go back to work in peace, guilt free."

Mom wasn't exactly the kind of person who fussed and spoiled us, but she was the kind of mother who every once in a while got the guilts because she didn't. Either way, she was all right. Daddy didn't seem to mind that she had decided to stay in the city this summer, but I knew he wouldn't mind it either when she'd come out and fuss over him. I even looked forward to seeing her a little, but I kind of thought it would be good for her to come for an hour or so and then head back home. Not so, my mother. She was coming out for a few days. Open end. Till she convinced herself that we didn't need her. Only then would she go home.

I stood looking out the back door. The hollyhock stems were heavy with green buds. "When's she coming?"

"Tonight."

Not till tonight. I thought of the Pridley and the bike ride, but suddenly I felt a little shy, a little frightened to go by myself, like I wouldn't be sure what to say to Brendan, and what if he asked me to go water-skiing with him and Sammy? I'd feel funny being the only girl. I looked over at the Silvers'. All was quiet. It could wait. She'd come over sooner or later and then it would be a little easier.

"What were your plans for the rest of the day, Pepper? Anything special?" Daddy was stirring his coffee and buttoning up his woolen shirt, ready to go back to work.

"Oh, I don't know. Think I'll just hang around and see

if I can work up some real serious boredom. That way Mom'll take one look at me and run us over to Harborville to buy me some new clothes or something."

"Sounds ingenious," he said. "If you want to get really bored, why don't you straighten up around here, and maybe run some dishes through the suds. That way we'll show Mom we can manage here like normal humans, and *also* you'll get bored! It's perfect." He sighed and smiled at me. "You know, that's the best material I've come up with today! You inspire me, Pep. Why don't you come in and curl at my feet, look up at me with your goony eyes, so the muses don't leave me?"

I gave him my you-gotta-be-kidding look. "I think Lois is better at that than I am," I told him as I opened the screen door. "I'll be seeing you. I've got my own ideas on how to get bored." And with that I stepped out onto the back step into the harsh sunlight. I broke a fat hollyhock blossom off its stem and sat on the step and slowly tore it up until my fingers were yellow and sweet-smelling.

I thought about how Simone had probably never washed a dish in her entire life. And how if I were her, I'd never be bored. But on second thought, maybe I'd *always* be bored. Everything might bore me. Why I'd bet even having my name up on an expressway overpass would be boring. If I were Simone.

Simone

Father sits at one end of the table. The late-afternoon light through the lacy curtain casts a strange shadow across his face. He looks as if he's been crying. But Father doesn't cry. Even as a child, a baby, I'm sure he never cried. He was born, looked around, and then picked up his *Wall Street Journal*. He is fearless, cold, but always polite.

He looks at me. "How was your shopping excursion, Simone?" he asks. But Mother answers.

"Wonderful! Christine had some lovely little designs she'd brought back from her trip to Paris last week, and they fit Simone perfectly. They look marvelous, don't they, dear?" She makes an awkward maneuver with her fork, and it flies from her hand and shoots across the table and onto the floor. Father and I ignore it.

"Yes, they're nice," I answer, cutting myself short with a sip of water from my crystal glass.

"Ramona!" Mother calls through her teeth. "Where is she?"

Ramona whisks through the doorway from the kitchen and is immediately at Mother's side. "Yes, Mrs. Silver?"

"A fork."

"Yes, ma'am." Ramona looks puzzled, and I know she thinks she has forgotten to set the table properly and leaves to get another.

Father coughs. He coughs at interesting moments. And sometimes I sense his little "ahem" is a throw cover he tosses over moments he doesn't like. Little punctuation marks that cover up and start again.

"And the Jaguar? Did you have any problems?" he asks her.

"None, except I guess I should tell you, we got a ticket double parking outside Tiffany's." She takes a long gulp of her water and then stares at it, probably surprised it's not wine. Yesterday afternoon she said she was on a health kick—no more liquor. She's had two drinks since then. They don't count.

"A ticket?"

"Yes, it was absurd," she says, snapping a fork from Ramona's hand. "How can you get anything out of the store if you can't park near there? I was just going to get the doorman to help me put the new china in the trunk, and the next thing I knew—"

"Mother. We couldn't *find* you. The doorman put the stuff in the trunk and you were gone."

"I only went back to pick up one thing real quick. I remembered the Whitfields' anniversary dinner next week, and I thought as long as I was there I'd pick up a little silver something or other—"

"A half hour, Mother. I was sure they were going to tow us. I thought you'd gone for a cocktail."

Father coughs.

Mother's eyes narrow. "How can you say that to me?" she says slowly, threateningly. "You of all people know how hard I'm trying. Ramona!" she screams. "A fork!"

Ramona hurries back and looks at my mother. "It's in your hand, ma'am."

Mother looks at her fork stupidly. "I mean Soave. Bring me some chilled Soave. And take this water glass away."

"Yes, ma'am." Ramona's eyes are downcast, but I catch the slightest flicker of dark brown as they glance at Father and away. She leaves.

" I thought you were on a health kick," I say.

"What's the point?" she asks, her voice trembly with tears and weakness. "If you're going to think I'm drinking when I'm not, I might as well drink and enjoy myself."

"Mother says you've made friends with Mintz's daughter," Father says out of nowhere.

I stare at him. Is this fury or courage I feel? "Don't you hate when she drinks?" I ask him quietly.

He is a face looking out at me from a movie screen. Talking to me, not hearing me. "Have you seen her since you got back from the city?"

"Who?" I ask.

"Mintz's daughter."

I guess it's fury. It leaves me so quickly, leaves me so

limp and empty. "No. I haven't seen her." I put some fish in my mouth. It's cold.

Ramona brings in the bottle of white wine, pours a glass in front of mother, and whisks away her water glass.

"Thank you, dear," my mother says to her.

Mother becomes a black hole. I see everything in the room and at the table except her. She is blocked out. I don't even listen to what she is saying, which is suddenly soft and coaxing.

"May I be excused?" I ask my father.

"Answer your mother," he says kindly.

"Thank you." I am just like him. I crumple my linen napkin next to my plate. I pretend he has said yes and I leave the table.

"Simone—" Mother whines.

The porch looks out at the bay, and the sky is so full of hundreds of little wispy clouds that I know the sunset will be spectacular tonight. I sit on one of the pale-pink chairs and wait. I twist my promise bracelet around my wrist, the one made of string and shells like Adilia taught me. I promise myself I'll get out of this soon. I promise myself a different life.

Almost in answer there's the sound of an engine, a rubber-band kind of engine, choking and sputtering, and a pale-blue Volkswagen heads up our drive toward the house. I think it must be Ramona's husband come for her early, but there are two people, guys. It's the two from the

Pridley. Ali's Brendan and his friend Sammy. I go to the railing to watch them, and they pull right alongside the house near me.

Sammy speaks first. "Hi."

"Hi." I answer, an octave lower.

"Where's your friend?" Brendan asks across Sammy through the open window.

"She lives over there." I motion with my chin toward the cottage.

Brendan has gotten out of the car and stands there leaning on the roof. He *is* nice. He's grinning at me. "You two want to go to the fireworks? We're just heading over there now."

I don't know if I feel safe leaving, with Mother drinking and angry. Maybe she'll do some more coke. Besides, I don't like to seem so available. "I'm not sure—"

"Of course she'll go!" It's Father behind me, *The Wall Street Journal* in his hand.

"Father—"

"You go off now with your friends, Simone. You've been with your mother for days. You need to be with young people."

"I have to get dressed," I say, looking down at my halter and shorts.

"You're just fine." Sammy laughs. "This is a come-as-you-are fireworks display."

"Go ahead, Simone," Father says. "Get dressed if you

must." He turns to the car. Here it comes. "What kind of car have you got there, boys? Think it will make it through the night?"

I go into the house to the sound of their laughter, and return in jeans and a big shirt to find them snug and beaming in Father's old Porsche. Brendan's in the driver's seat. Sammy's in the back. "I told them to take the Porsche," Father whispers to me, beaming. "I don't want to worry about my little girl breaking down anywhere."

Like it's always been. I remember being little and the friends I had who always wanted to play with me—not with me, but with the child-size Noah's ark I had in my playroom. Then there were the couple of friends who knew they'd go to Antigua with me for the holidays if they were around enough. And now two summer boys smile up at me from the leather upholstery of my father's Porsche. Oh, they love me, they love me, all right. I get in and slam the door. Sounds like money. Slowly we pull out of the driveway, past the garden. The fennel smells rich and pungent tonight.

Ali

I was helping Mom unpack when I heard the horn beep outside. I figured it was one of Daddy's friends to pick him up for a meeting, and I was busy noticing that she had brought only two changes of clothes—good, she wasn't planning on interfering on Paradise Island for too long—when Daddy called into the bedroom.

"Ali! Looks like some young people here for you. The Silver girl and a couple of guys."

"Huh!" Mom said, smiling at me. "Doesn't sound boring at all."

"Told you," I said.

Before I had the thought to compose myself and be cool and relaxed, I raced across the living room, through the kitchen, burst out the screen door. There on the blue stone driveway was a beautiful old silver sports car. Brendan was driving, Sammy was folded in the back, and Simone was sitting high on the back of the front seat, smoking a cigarette and looking for all the world like an ad for diamond-studded jeans. Is this where she'd been for the last few days? Off with Brendan and Sammy by herself?

"Hey, Ali," Brendan called. I was in sweatpants and a faded T-shirt. I should have stayed behind the door, filtered out by the screen. "Want to go to see some fireworks tonight in Aquebogue? Hottest show on the east end. They use some farmer's old potato field."

Sammy was smiling. "That's right," he explained. "They set potatoes on fire, throw them in the air, and then they shoot them. When they blow up, it's almost like the real thing! There's no topping these east enders—they'll stop at nothing to please."

Simone blew a stream of smoke into the air. "Come on," she coaxed. "It's not Grucci, but it's not bad. I've seen them before." She dropped from her perch and slid over close to Brendan to make room for me. As if whether or not I went depended on the megatons of the display.

"Okay," I said. "Okay. Let me just tell my parents."

In the stretch of three minutes, I changed from my sweatpants and T-shirt to my jeans and a baggy cotton shirt, switched my running shoes for my flats, ran a brush through my hair, dabbed some blush on my cheeks, some gloss on my mouth, and yelled, "Goodbyeseeyoulater-I'mgoingnow."

"Just a minute, young lady," like a 45 record suddenly switched to 33. I ground to a halt at the door, poised to split, not wanting to do the parent scene. Mom had come out of her room. "Who are these people and where are you going?"

"What's this, an English essay?" I asked. "You want motivations and subplots, too?"

"Pepper," warned Daddy in a deep voice.

I took a breath and dropped my hand from the door. "It's Simone, the Silvers' daughter, and two guys from the Pridley that we met. They're friends of Frank's—you know, Daddy, that guy with the mustache at the Harborville meeting."

My parents were coming closer to me, to the door, looking out at the car. Lois joined in, only she nudged the door open, walked right up to the car, and stood on her hind legs, smiling in at them. Probably just what my parents wanted to do themselves. Before I knew it, we were all out on the back stoop.

Sammy opened the door and Lois climbed in. The three of them were laughing. Lois was in her glory. "Come on, folks, pile in," Sammy called. "We're off to the fireworks!"

"Fireworks?" Dad said. "Where's that? On Dune Island tonight?"

"No," Sammy answered. "Over in Aquebogue. On a potato farm. They set these potatoes on—"

Brendan cuffed him playfully. "What do you want? Everyone to think this is a cheap date? Aquebogue got the leftover fireworks from Monte Carlo this year," he pretended to my parents, "and we thought Ali and Simone here would like to see them. That's all. Simple."

My parents were smiling. I made introductions as I tried to pull Lois out of the car. Mom slipped her hand in Lois' collar and held her back. "Well, don't be too late," she said.

"What?" I asked. "Two o'clock?"

"Twelve."

"Ma!"

"Twelve thirty."

I stared at my father.

"One," he said. "By the time it gets dark and you get the ferry back and all. . . ."

"Just a minute," Mom called, and she jogged back into the house.

"Great car, Brendan," my father said, smoothing his hand over the rounded fender.

"It's the Silvers'," Brendan answered, shrugging. "Her father insisted we take it when he got a load of my car."

Mom came back with a big afghan and tucked it in the back of the seat next to Sammy. "Okay, kids," she called, backing up. "Have a great time. And be careful."

"Watch out for flying hot potatoes tonight!" Sammy called back to them as we drove off, with Lois following us halfway up the drive.

Simone and I were pressed up against each other, arm to arm, leg to leg. I looked at her, felt her look away, and looked away myself. Why couldn't this have been anybody else except the princess of Dune Island, for pete's sakes? What made me so lucky?

"So," she said over the roar of the engine and the wind of the convertible. "How've you been?"

"I've been fine," I answered. "And you?"

"Lousy. Had to go with my mother into the city for a few days. Shopping. I hate it."

So that's where she was. "Where'd you pick up these two island boys?" I teased, loud enough for them to hear, but I really wanted an answer.

Simone shrugged. "Same place you found them. In my yard. Sniffing around. Looking for us."

Us? Looking for both of us? I relaxed a little. We were on equal ground here. I was relieved to know she'd been away and hadn't been hanging around with Brendan and Sammy the last few days, after I'd been too shy myself to go alone.

"Yeah, we hadn't seen you around," Brendan said, leaning forward and looking past Simone at me. "First we were looking for you just to see if you wanted to go water-skiing Friday, if we saw you at the Pridley again, and then we found out about the fireworks, and well, we hadn't seen you, so we decided to take things into our own hands."

Simone leaned forward suddenly to light a cigarette and blocked him from my view. "Fireworks, yes. Water-skiing, no," she said under her breath. I don't think Brendan heard her, and when I leaned back slightly to see him, he smiled at me. I swear his smile went from his eyes to my eyes to someplace deep in my stomach. I didn't need skiis, a motorboat, water—I was skimming along, flying.

That was the way the whole night went—all friendly and happy, and every time Brendan's eyes met mine, it felt like trucks colliding on the interstate to me. Although I couldn't begin to guess what he was feeling, I was sure I was falling in love. Even today I get a little jittery remembering how he looked, all open-faced and touchable there in that dark potato field with fireworks sparkling like Christmas decorations in his big eyes.

It's funny, but looking back on that night, with all its strong feelings and experiences with Brendan, my clearest memories have more to do with Simone than with him. There was something about her that night. I still can't describe it. It was like a vibration, as if a gong had just gone off somewhere deep inside her. She was happy and all, friendlier than usual even, maneuvering me to sit next to Brendan on the afghan, dragging Sammy off to buy some hot dogs. Maybe it was that she never really looked at me, never made eye contact, or something that subtle, that indescribable. She talked and joked and laughed, but I think she would have been exactly the same even if she had been totally alone. She was a soap opera actress, saying her lines, making her moves, but reading the cue cards over our shoulders and never looking at us.

And coming home on the ferry, she really got strange. As soon as Mr. Silver's Porsche was in park, we hopped out of it and ran to the railing to watch Dune Island, sprinkled with lights, approach in the night. It was cooler now, dark as could be, and so beautiful. The sky was like an upturned bowl over us, so round and full of starlight.

"Come on, Simone," Sammy called back to the car. And it was then I realized she hadn't come along with us to the railing. I watched as she slowly opened the door, and then I turned back to the emptiness ahead, feeling the ferry drift away from the dock and start home. The last ferry. We had made it. Brendan and Sammy were talking about the heavy currents the ferry had to ride through, about inlets, and where to go fishing, pointing off to indistinct spots along the dark shore that they knew so well.

I looked at Simone as she came up alongside me. She raised her hand to her face and rubbed her eye. I saw she was trembling.

"Cold?" I asked her.

"No," she answered in a low voice, just to me. "Spooked."

"Yeah," I agreed. "This is weird, isn't it? So silent, and dark."

"I usually wait in the car when I have to come across at night."

"Aw, that's no fun. Real fun would be to climb over this railing and stand out on the prow. Wouldn't it?" I looked over my shoulder at the ferryman high in his steering place. "I don't think that old guy'd like it very much, though."

She said something so low I couldn't hear her.

"What?"

Again the lowest voice. "I saw someone drown off the side of this ferry one night."

"Oh, God!" I thought of falling into this black churning water. I imagined unspeakable things biting at me, the undertow pulling me down, under the ferry, into the ferry blades. "How could such a thing happen?" I asked. "It's not like this is a rough ride and you'd get thrown off the ferry or anything."

"No. I saw her walk off. She walked right off the side."

I knew Brendan and Sammy were quiet, listening now.

"That must have been awful," Sammy said. "I'd never heard anything about that around here."

"Oh, it was a long time ago," Simone said, her voice more normal now, her trembling hands gripped to stillness on the rail. "I was little, maybe seven or eight, I guess."

"Jeez," Brendan said beneath his breath. "How do you explain a suicide to a kid that little?"

Simone's head snapped around. "It *wasn't* suicide!" she snapped. There was a hard thrust to her chin, and the whites of her eyes suddenly glowed red in the dim light of the ferry deck.

His hands went up in immediate surrender. "Okay. Okay. Don't get bent. Whatever you say." And then to smooth the moment, sensing her sudden panic, he slipped his arm around her neck in an affectionate headlock and joked with her. "Just don't yell at *me*, Princess. You don't know who you're dealing with here."

I saw her lower her eyes and smile sheepishly. Her hand came up and wrapped around his wrist. And we all started to laugh. I guess we were laughing for all different reasons, out of our own distinct reactions, and God only knows why *I* was laughing—Brendan standing there with his arm around the princess of Dune Island after making eyes at me all night. But we laughed all right, and the ferry kept barreling right along through the currents. Taking us all home.

Simone

"Have you got them?" I ask her.

In the yellow light of sunrise Ali holds out her hands to me. She has brought seven hollyhock blossoms like I told her. They are new, though, and their powder is still sparse and locked firmly to their stamens. The powder won't shake off. We'll have to scrape it off.

"This is so exciting." She whispers, even though we are at the side of West Neck Road and no one is around for miles. All I can hear are the seabirds, gathering their breakfast on the sand. "What did *you* bring?"

I hold up the stems, but she doesn't recognize them. "Fennel," I remind her.

"Where did you learn all this?"

"Oh, I knew someone once who had the Gift," I say. "She taught me some things."

"The Gift," she says reverently. "I love it! But what are you going to do?"

"See the future. Make an oath."

"Can you contact the dead? I have this grandmother who was really great—"

"No." I answer sharply. What does she think this is, a parlor trick? A magic act? I start down to the water, with my doubts, like I always have with her.

"Wait," she calls. "Why don't we do it right here, on top of this boulder?" I look back to see her climbing up, her hair loose around her face, the hollyhock on the ground. "Rocks have magic," she calls, "like Stonehenge, you know, stuff like that. On top of this rock at sunrise. It would be great."

She is so foolish. Even as a child I knew not to question Adilia, to just follow her. "Don't forget to bring the hollyhock," I call over my shoulder. The water is so clear and quiet, thin lines of white waves tracing scoops along the shoreline, rocks glistening, shells crunching under my feet. I hear Ali running up behind me.

"Simone, wait up. I don't know if it's such a good idea to be here. It says no trespassing back on the road."

"It's Bootleggers' Cove," I tell her. "*Bootleggers*, Ali. You're *supposed* to trespass here. It's a tradition."

"Are you sure? I hate to do stuff like this. . . ."

"Quiet," I say. And I stand there, very still, my toes at the edge of the pulsing water, my eyes on the horizon knife. Waiting. Waiting. For an instant I recall my mother sleeping on the porch chair this morning. I smell the liquor still clinging to me, to my mind, to my clothes. But I wait, breathe slowly, and then, yes, I begin to feel Adilia all around me. Her song laps at my feet, her cocoa breath brushes my arm. I hold the feeling. "All right now," I say. "Let's find a place to sit." We turn back to the shore, to a spot that is slightly sunken near a dune, and with my feet I smooth a place in the sand, a circle big enough for the two of us.

The sand is still cool, and we sit facing each other. The fennel beside me, the hollyhock beside her; and now from the pouch of my sweatshirt, I draw out my silk-covered tarot cards, unwind the pale scarf, and spread it out on the sand in a square between us. I place the cards in the center. Their colors are vibrant and deep in this light.

"Oh, how beautiful," Ali says, not touching them.

"Go ahead," I tell her, and she takes them with both hands as though they were made of blown glass. "Shuffle them, and while you're shuffling, think of a question you'd like the answer to. Any question about the past, present, or future. One that needs only a yes or no answer."

"Okay," she says slowly. Awkwardly she stretches her fingers around them and tries to shuffle. "The future. The future, what I want to know, let me see, if I had one question—"

"Shhh. Don't tell me. Just be quiet, and think it to yourself."

Adilia would wait patiently. Watch her shuffle eight, nine times. Gaze over her head at the bay, smooth her apron, pat her brown cotton-candy hair behind her ear.

"There," Ali says. She holds them out to me.

"Now with your left hand," I tell her, "place the cards on the scarf and cut it into three piles to your left."

Three even piles, and with my right hand I pick them up, from my left. I hold them in both hands, pray for answers, ask for truth and seeing and good events. Then I lay out the top five cards—"Today, yesterday, tomorrow, ago, and to be." They are all upside down. Not good. Terrible as a matter of fact. Should I lie?

I glance at her, she glances at me. It's too late. She's read my face.

"What's wrong?"

"The answer to your question is a definite, positive, no."

Ali throws back her head and laughs. "Oh, thank God! Thank you, thank you, thank you."

"But . . . what was your question?"

"I asked if I was going to be a virgin for the rest of my life." She throws herself back on the sand, laughing.

I pick up the cards. This isn't working right. I shuffled them once to erase the nonsense, and she sits up again.

"You're not doing this right," I tell her. "Shuffle them again, only this time ask a question that the yes will be happy, not the no. Ask so it's positive."

"What about you?" she asks.

"What *about* me?"

"Have you had sex yet?"

"Is that what you want me to ask the cards? Has Simone had sex yet?"

"Simone, cut it out. Are you a virgin? I told *you*."

"Technically."

"Technically! What does that mean? Technically."

"It means that if a doctor examined me, he'd say I was a virgin, but I'm hardly inexperienced. Here, would you please shuffle."

She takes the cards but sits there staring at me. "Huh."

I stare back at her.

"That sounds interesting," she says quietly, beginning to shuffle. "I'm afraid I'm an across the board, technically and untechnically, specifically and broadly, a virgin."

"That won't last."

"I guess not."

"Are you thinking of a question?"

"No. All right. Let me concentrate."

I wait again, staring out at the water until she has cut the cards. I gather them up. "You've thought of a question?"

She nods, her question locked inside.

I lay them out once more—"Today, yesterday, tomorrow, ago, and to be." Only two are upside down. And here is Ali's card, "today," the Queen of Wands, with her hair in a long braid. The good queen. The queen who always has things go her way. "This is you," I say, pointing to the Queen. "She's lucky in everything. And see the sunflower? She's close to nature."

"That's me all right—Nature Girl. But what's the answer to my question?"

"It's yes, most likely, yes. See. Three are right side up. That's good."

"What's this one?" She points to the Hanged Man, who is upside down. I'm glad she doesn't ask about the Eight of Cups. Adilia would shake her head slowly and rumble inside over that one.

"That's in the future spot. Not tomorrow but further away. Something will happen. And you won't follow your intuition. You'll think too much."

"And all the blood will go to my head, like that guy, right?"

Somehow I know she's not serious. I gather up the cards. "What was your question?"

"I thought I'm not supposed to tell you."

"You can tell me at the end of the reading. It's important for me to know what it is, so I can see it happen and know the cards were right."

Her face gets all quizzical and soft. "I'm embarrassed," she says.

"What's to be embarrassed about? You already said you were a virgin. After that, anything's downhill."

"I asked the cards if you and I would ever be good friends."

"We *are* good friends," I say too fast. I remind myself for some reason of my mother, the way she says, "Yes, I love you, darling," and then rifles through her pocketbook for her mirror, or the way she rolls her eyes while she talks on the phone, her expression the flip side of her voice that's syrupy and gracious.

"No, we're not."

Ali surprises me, saying we're not friends as we sit here at seven in the morning. Who else would I do this with if not a friend? Maybe she doesn't like me after all.

"Not *good* friends, anyway," she goes on. "Maybe we will be, eventually. But I don't know. Time will tell."

I don't know why I say it. I regret it as it passes my lips. I don't know how to talk like this, to talk to some-one about our friendship, as though it were a bowl of fruit between us. It's almost a whisper. "You're my only friend."

"Yeah, me, too," she answers, not really understanding. "This place is hardly Bikini Beach. I mean I can't think of one other teenage girl I've seen the whole time. Have you? It's just you and me, Princess. Kind of like the last two survivors, you know?"

"We can agree to be friends," I suggest. I wind the silk around the cards. No more questions. No more answers.

"Well, yeah, we are friends, I guess. But I don't know." She lies down on her back and looks out at the bay.

"We can make promise bracelets," I say.

"Is that what you're wearing?" She turns and looks at the bracelet on my wrist.

"Yes. These are special shells here, especially along

Bootleggers' Cove, and I know a way to string them to make bracelets that we can wear all summer. Never take them off. And we'll make an oath on them, and do some magic on them, so the oath will be strong and lasting."

"Oaths, like what?"

"Well, for instance, I can make an oath to do everything in my power to help you win Brendan this summer."

She smiles. "You won't pay him to call me, will you?"

"Of course not."

"What's the promise in *that* bracelet?" she asks, motioning to the one already on my arm.

"I can't say once the oath has been made. It loses its power that way. This one I made alone. I can't tell you."

"And what oath do I get to make?"

I pretend I am just now making it up, but I have thought about it for days. "Well, let me see. Your oath to me can be . . . I know. You can promise to never go water-skiing this summer. If the guys bring it up again, just pretend you hate it. You don't want to go."

She looks at me hard. "Why don't *you* just say you don't want to go?"

I run my fingers through my hair, looking away from her. "I just don't want to. I don't like standing on the water. I don't want to have to explain it. Will you do it or not?"

Ali is quiet. I feel like I've given her such a fragile part of me, and that if she refuses, I couldn't bear knowing she carries that part of me for all time. But she doesn't seem to really understand. "All right, now, so what is it? You promise to help me get Brendan to fall in love with me this summer, and I promise to pretend to hate water-skiing. That's it?"

"Basically."

She shrugs. "Okay, so what do we do?"

I show Ali how to collect the right shells, the pale yellow-pink jingle shells with round holes in them. She walks along the beach with me, chattering, silly, not even noticing that I am barely breathing. I force myself not to cry. I miss Adilia so. And think of her now, so strongly—how she had done her magic and taught me how to string the shells. That day on the beach, I had promised her I would try with all my might to not wet my bed at night anymore. And somehow it had worked. But Adilia had promised to walk on water for me. Right on the bay, she had said. When the time was right.

When our hands and pockets are full of jingle shells, I show Ali how to make a pile of them up on the sand. It is very still and bright now. I show her how to scrape the flower stamens and sprinkle the hollyhock powder over the pile, and then we each take a turn twisting the fennel over the pile so that tiny leaves sprinkle down over it, speaking our promises as we do. The hollyhock should make the promises easy to keep, but the fennel—and I don't tell her this—will let me back out later, if I can't keep the promise, if it turns out to be too hard.

"And no more lies," she says as we begin to gather up the shells to string them.

"Right," I answer, "no more lies." But I keep my eyes down, looking at the shells. I cannot look at her right now.

Ali

I was right. My mother couldn't wait to take me into Harborville to do a little shopping. As she drove the car off the ferry on the Harborville side, the little town opened up before us like a picture on a calendar—the cobblestone streets, the brick sidewalks, the shops, the old-fashioned lights. It was a nice combination of quaint and clean modern, a town that kind of promised you there was not a thing wrong in the whole entire world.

We parked right around the corner from the church where Daddy's AA group met and decided to systematically work one side of the street, stop for lunch, and make our way down the other side.

"So tell me," Mom began. "What's this Simone girl like?"

I shrugged. "I'm not sure. Sometimes she's a real snot, putting on airs, like with her servants and her clothes, and all her experiences, and other times she seems like she's about four years old and on the verge of falling apart."

"What do you mean?"

"Oh, I don't know. It's just she's a little unusual, that's

all. Don't worry about it. She's okay. In a way she's nice."
I turned the promise bracelet around my wrist and thought
of her oath. "Yeah, she's okay."

"I don't know, Ali. I really don't like the idea of you
having all this free time out here, with Daddy busy all
the time, and the only girl your age seems to think she's
thirty years old."

I laughed. "What makes you say that?"

"The hair, the nails, the look. Whatever happened to
being sixteen and carefree? Good grooming is one thing,
but she's polished to a high sheen. Like that's all she
does."

"That's not all she does. Come on."

"Well, then, what *does* she do? What are her interests?"

What could I tell my mother? Witchcraft? Magic herb
gardening? Lying? Men? She'd pack my bags in a split
second. "Well, she runs. She's a good jogger, better than
I am. And she swims—"

"Works on her tan."

"She gardens." I wouldn't dare tell her about the marijuana in the Silvers' yard.

"Gardens! With those fingernails?"

"Mom!" I stopped in the middle of the sidewalk. "Stop
it. She's my friend. Why are you doing this?"

"I'm sorry. You're right," she admitted, slipping her
arm through mine and moving me along. "It's just I've
never been away from you a whole summer like this, and
I worry."

"Well, stop worrying already. You're getting nasty."

"Are you sure you wouldn't want to come home with me? There's a painting workshop at the high school. It's not too late to sign up for it. We could hit a movie now and then."

"You know what I think, Mom?"

"What?"

"I think you're just lonely."

She was quiet. She stopped at a store window and looked at a dress displayed on an elegant mannequin. She stared at it. "You're right, you know. I miss you guys."

"But aren't you busy? You said you had so much work to do on the dissertation and it would be perfect, these weeks alone."

"Yes, yes. That's all true, but at the end of the day, I get lonely. I lift my head out of the books and I look around and no one's there. Not even Lois."

"Why don't you take Lois back with you then?"

"I wouldn't want to do that. This is so good for her out here. She can romp around and have all this freedom."

"It's good for me out here, too, Mom."

"Yes, I know. I can see that. You look good. Your color is nice, and your hair's shining, and you've even stopped biting your nails."

"You noticed."

"Of course I did." Mom smiled at me, the kind of smile that if she were Lois, she'd sniff all around my face.

"If you get lonely at night," I said, "why don't you go to an open AA meeting. That's what we do."

Mom squeezed me quick and laughed. "That doesn't work quite for me the way it does for Daddy, but you're right. Maybe I'll stop down at the Steppingstone group and say hello to Edith and Marilyn. Haven't talked to anyone in so long. Just my dissertation advisor, and Dr. Arroyo is hardly a brilliant conversationalist."

"And why don't you call Gram, too? Or Maureen—"

Two people came out of the dress shop and we began to move to get out of the way.

"Hi, Ali." It was Simone. She was standing there with a woman I somehow knew was her mother. What a strange meeting. I knew I was quite a different person with my mother than I was with Simone, and I'm sure it was the same for Simone, yet here we were, all four of us, converging right on the doorway of the dress shop.

"Oh, hi, Simone. This is my mother, Carole Mintz. Mom, this is Simone—"

"And this is my mother, Rebecca Silver."

Mrs. Silver's face lit up. She wasn't as pretty as Simone. I was surprised. I thought she'd be more glamorous, more polished, more everything, but she was sort of skinny and haggard-looking—dressed to the teeth, I mean jewels and soft leather, but her eyes lacked something that Simone's had too much of.

"How nice to meet you at last," she said. "I called the

cottage when your husband first arrived and invited him over for drinks with my husband and me, but he insisted he was working, and not socializing. I've never known a writer before. Do they really do that?"

"Charlie does." My mother laughed.

"But of course," Mrs. Silver pushed, "now that you're here, he'll come. You must."

Mom shrugged. "I'm only out here for a couple of days, and he barely notices. He's very intense right now. And not the greatest of company."

"He's kind of spacy," I added.

"Well, then you'll certainly join Simone and me for lunch now, won't you? We were just saying how hungry we were, weren't we, dear?"

Oh, no, I thought. Not lunch. Not a whole long lunch with mothers.

"That would be nice," my mother said. Without even asking me. Without even thinking that I might hate it. She'd tell me I was like my father. Well, I knew she was hungry for talk and people. Oh, well, so what. How long could a lunch be? She was probably dying to see what Simone was like, too. I just hoped she wouldn't force me to go back home with her by the time lunch was over.

"Follow us," Mrs. Silver said, leading the way up the block. "The Harbor has the best seafood, and the most divine ladies' salads."

Simone and I looked at each other. Ladies' salads? I

mouthed. I frowned and Simone's lips twitched into the smallest, smuggest smile.

The Harbor was exactly the kind of restaurant that never would have occurred to Mom or me to stop in. I mean they had lace curtains on the long windows and a maitre d'. "Good day, Mrs. Silver," he said. "Your usual table?"

"Yes, Clinton. By the window, please."

We followed him through the restaurant, our footsteps muffled in thick carpeting, and all light and noise absorbed into the heavy brocaded walls. I saw Mom check in her pocketbook and flick through her bills. In the back room a broad window opened out onto West Neck Harbor. A small fleet of white sailboats was moving slowly along.

The maitre d' helped Mrs. Silver into her chair, and then Mom. I slipped into my seat quickly. "A cocktail, Carole?" Mrs. Silver asked.

"No, thank you," my mother answered.

It seemed Mrs. Silver was going to say something to my mother. It flitted across her face, but then she just said, "Scotch on the rocks, Clinton."

Simone sighed and gazed out at the sailboats. Then she took a pack of cigarettes out of her pocketbook and lit up. I glanced at my mother. No reaction.

"So, our daughters seem to have struck up a friendship this summer," Mrs. Silver began. "Jogging and all."

"Yes. I've heard," Mom said. "And I just noticed Simone's lovely bracelets. They're just like the one you have, Ali."

"We made them," Simone said, extending her wrist to my mother, the cigarette poised between two long fingers.

"Oh, I think they're so hideous," Mrs. Silver said. "An old servant of ours once taught Simone how to make them when she was little, and she makes them every summer. I'd think you'd be a little old for them, darling. You have that nice ivory bracelet I got you in Saks. It's so much nicer."

"I never run out of shells," Simone said to my mother, not even acknowledging that Mrs. Silver had spoken. "Every summer the beach is full of them. I think if everyone took all they could carry, there'd still be more. I can't imagine where they come from. They're so flat." Simone placed her cigarette in the ashtray and examined the shells on her wrist carefully.

Clinton placed a heavy glass full of amber liquor and glistening ice by Mrs. Silver's place and placed a thick menu before each of us. I swear, it seems that I picked up the menu to look at it, opened it up, and the next time I looked, within seconds, Mrs. Silver's glass was nearly drained. I looked at Mom, but she was studying the menu.

Simone turned to look out the window at the bay, and I thought she whispered something under her breath to her mother. Mrs. Silver seemed not to hear, but stared straight ahead, her face tight and hard.

"The lobster salad is wonderful here, Carole. And lunch is on my husband. We'll just put it on his account—"

"Oh, I don't know," Mom said, laughing nervously.

"Please," Mrs. Silver ordered. "I insist. Clinton. Another scotch, please." To Simone she whispered hoarsely, "Stop it," and Mom and I pretended we hadn't noticed.

Lunch was a disaster. If Simone had been laundry on a line, and Mrs. Silver had been a big black crow, Simone would have been torn to shreds by the time the last of the lobster had been eaten. Everything Mom tried to talk about turned into ammunition to criticize Simone. All with good humor, and all tongue-in-cheek but also blade-in-gut. Mrs. Silver's hard tight face grew looser and softer as lunch went on, Clinton refreshing her drink, and Simone just sitting there in her glassy beauty, bored, detached, and constantly distracted by the scattered boat activity out on the bay.

When our mothers got up to go to the ladies' room, (Mom had already refused coffee and any chance to linger), Simone and I stared each other down. I felt like she was poised to catch something I was about to throw at her. I thought, What the hell?

"She's smashed," I said, quietly.

Simone just looked at me. I think she was surprised I had said it right out like that. "She certainly is." Again the boats, the bay. She had eaten very little.

"Why don't you tell her to get help?" I asked.

"Me? Tell her to get help? Are you kidding? I don't

have the sense to put my shoes on right in the morning. Why should she listen to me?"

"Tell her how her drinking is hurting you."

"Get off it, Ali." Simone smashed a freshly lit cigarette in the ashtray.

"But that's all she does is hurt you."

"And you've only seen the tip of the iceberg, so butt out before you freeze. Okay?"

"What do you mean? Does she beat you? What do you mean?"

"No," she answered, throwing herself back against the seat. "She hurts herself more than anyone."

"How?"

She hesitated. "Drugs."

"You mean that grass in your garden?"

Simone laughed out loud. "That's play. American grass is weak, kind of like herb tea, you know? A joke. No, I mean real drugs."

"Illegal drugs?" I asked. How could we be talking like this? By all rights our mothers should be in the ladies' room discussing whether or not they thought their teenage daughters were experimenting with drugs. This was all backward.

"No," Simone snapped sarcastically. "Legal drugs, like Bayer aspirin and Robitussin. She really gets off on them."

I stared at her. She couldn't look at me. And then suddenly her voice was like a child's. Her eyes and the tip of her nose grew red. "I found her doing coke."

I immediately thought of all the health-class movies I had sat through, the lectures, the speakers who came from drug-addiction groups to talk to us about their recovery, and the ads on television—famous sports figures and rock stars saying "Don't do it." Jesus. Simone's mother.

"What are you going to do?"

"There's nothing to do."

"There must be something. You have to get help for her," I insisted. "Before she gets arrested or something."

"Ali." Her voice was suddenly threatening and sharp. "If you tell a soul, I will kill you. Swear to me."

"I won't tell anyone, Simone, but, my God—" I reached out to squeeze her hand, to reassure her, but Mrs. Silver's voice cut through the air as they approached.

"And this coming Saturday night, we're throwing our midsummer bash, and you absolutely must come. Besides, if you don't come, your old writer man won't get much work done anyway, with all that music and carrying on."

"I'd love to come, Rebecca," Mom lied politely, "but I'll be gone by Saturday, and I'm pretty sure Charlie made other arrangements for that night."

"Oh, now," Mrs. Silver said, pouting and flopping into her chair. "I thought he didn't do any socializing at all."

"Old friends," Mom said, smiling stiffly. She reached into her pocketbook, but Mrs. Silver seized the check and wouldn't surrender it. She moved like a wooden doll whose rubber-band joints had all dried up.

"Well, thank you," Mom said, "but we really must be going. Before it gets too late. We want to see as many shops as we can."

"I understand, dear," Mrs. Silver slurred. "You go on. Simone and I will just have some coffee before we head home."

Mom stood up and looked at me. "Ali?"

"It was nice meeting you, Mrs. Silver." I could lie, too. "I'll see you later, maybe, Simone, okay?"

"You come to the party Saturday night, dear," Mrs. Silver said, pointing at me. "So Simone will have some company."

Simone didn't look like she needed company. She looked like she needed some heavy-duty protection, like mounted police or something.

"Oh, that was so sad," Mom said, once we were out in the glaring sunlight.

"Sad!" I said. "I think it's disgusting. She was horrible."

"It's a disease, Ali."

"Well, then she should go see a doctor and get some help. There's no excuse."

"No? What if one of the symptoms of the disease is to not be able to see what you're doing?"

"Maybe we could get her to a meeting. Maybe I can tell her Daddy's in AA, and she can go to a meeting with him. Then Simone and I could go to open—"

"You can't break Dad's anonymity, Ali. That's up to him. And you know, it's really up to her whether or not she gets help. She doesn't seem to be hurting yet as far as I can see."

I thought of the cocaine. I might have told my mother then, had I not promised Simone I wouldn't.

"She seems really wrapped up in her scene," Mom went on. "She's got to hit some kind of bottom and decide for herself that she needs help. No one can do that for her."

We walked on quietly for a while. I had lost all my interest in shopping. I felt as if I'd just witnessed a car wreck. All I wanted to do was take Simone home, wrap her in an afghan, and give her hot tea. I felt like crying.

"Mom?" It began to well up in me. I wasn't sure I could say it.

"Yes?" She was peering into the window of a kite shop.

"Was Daddy ever like that?" I whispered.

She turned and looked at me, pried into my face with her mother eyes. "Yes," she said simply. "A lot like that."

"Could he ever get like that again?"

"I don't think so. Your father's got some solid-gold sobriety under his belt." She put her arm around me and drew me to her, and I started to cry right there on the sidewalk in the sunlight.

"It's so scary," I told her.

"It is. Yes," she said. "When it goes untreated like Mrs. Silver, it's a frightening thing to watch, but when it's treated, like Dad, it's hard to explain, but it's the most wonderful thing to watch. Like watching an oak tree grow. Slow and steady, but glorious. Absolutely glorious."

[115]

Mom wiped her palms across my cheeks and smiled. "Don't you worry about your dad. He's doing just fine."

"I know," I said, letting my face be wiped. Next thing I'd know, she'd spit on the corner of a handkerchief and wipe my mouth. I laughed. "You know what? Let's buy a kite. A really great one. And we'll fly it before you go back."

"Great idea," she said. She draped her arm around my shoulders and we walked into the kite shop like two old buddies.

Simone

I have drawn the blinds in my room to block out the light. My head hurts so much. Like a knife in each of my eyes. If I hold very still, I can almost pretend it isn't there. For a while. Then my eyes begin to throb, and I move. Shift. I must be dying. But I can't be dying. I've had this before and I never die. I keep living.

There's a rapid tap on my door. "Miss Simone?" Ramona says. "Telephone for you. A gentleman named Sammy."

"Thank you, Ramona." I sound to myself like I am speaking from under water. The phone is on my night table, its ring turned off. I fumble for it and the whole thing clatters to the floor, sending fresh stabs into my head.

"Hello?" I whisper into the mouthpiece.

"Simone? It's me, Sammy. Howrya doing?"

"Oh, I don't know. I have a little headache, so I was just lying down a minute, but I guess I'm okay. I'll live."

He laughs. "That's good. 'Cause Brendan and I wanted to know if you'd go water-skiing with us tomorrow. We've got the use of the boat, and no one's on."

Ali is my safety net. She'll never agree to go. "Sounds nice. Why don't you check with Ali though, and whatever she says is fine with me."

I hear the extension pick up in my house. "Simone, darling?"

Oh, no.

"Simone, why don't you ask your friend if he'd like to come to the party Saturday?"

"Mother—"

"Sammy," she says, "do come. And bring your friends. We want to fill the house and garden with people, young people, old people like me"—she laughs too loud—"and everyone! Everyone should come! Plenty of food and goodies, and dancing. We're having a band. Promise me you'll come, Sammy dear."

"Well . . . ah, sure . . . Mrs. Silver. If it's okay with Simone. . . ."

"Mother." I speak as if to a senile person, pressing my fingers hard to my aching eyes. "Hang up the phone."

"Fine, fine—" The line goes dead.

"Sorry," I say. I don't know why. I'm not sorry. I'm humiliated. Furious.

"Listen, don't worry about it. Parents! I know all about them. They're all nuts."

"Yes. I guess so. Some more than others."

"But you'll come water-skiing tomorrow?" he continues.

"I don't see why not," I say, knowing Ali will think of something. And then I'll owe her one. Brendan. "Sammy?

Why *don't* you come Saturday night with Brendan? We don't have to get involved with my parents' friends. We've got a pool table in the basement, a stereo, dart board. We can have our own party."

"Sounds great. Okay. I'll get back to you. Let me call Ali and see what we can do tomorrow. You check in with her for when and where, all right?"

"Fine. And remind her about the party Saturday night," I tell him. "Tell her you and Brendan are coming."

"Got it," he says, and hangs up.

By then this headache will be gone. It never lasts more than a day. I imagine myself walking around Saturday without these knives embedded in my eyes. Such relief. I lay my splitting head on the pillow and the knives stab along the back of my neck and I close my eyes. Sleep is the only thing.

When I wake up it is dark. The headache lags. It has lost its sharpness. I lie here, wondering what time it is. Is it ten o'clock, or three o'clock? I have no idea. I just lie here, and then I hear music and a car outside. In the driveway. Slowly, I slide from my bed and peek out the window. I see that old convertible pulling away. The one with the radio. The one that was here the night I found mother with the cocaine.

I bolt from the window and fly out of my room. "Don't do it!" I scream from the top of the stairs. "Don't do it, you hear me?" I pound down the stairs, the blood rushing to my face, the headache building, every part of me trembling and hysterical.

Mother is at the bottom of the steps, looking subdued, innocent. "Simone! Hush! You'll wake everyone. What's the matter with you?"

"What was that car?" I shout.

"What car? Be quiet! You'll wake your father."

"You know what car. That junkie's car. That old convertible that just left."

"Come in here, Simone," she says, leading the way into the living room. "You're going to wake the dead." She sits on the sofa and pats the cushion beside her, and I sit there. "I don't know what car you're talking about, dear. You know sometimes people turn around in our drive when they're lost on this road." She brushes her hand across my forehead. "How's your headache?" she asks.

I don't see any paper bags, no straws. She seems relaxed, quiet. Why is she like this sometimes, so soft and approachable? Is this after fifteen drinks? Or seven and a half? Whatever it is, why can't she just reach this state all the time and stay here? I can tell she's freshly bathed. The ends of her curls are wet. She smells like flowers, and I start to breathe easier.

"Headache's still there," I tell her. "Please, Mother, don't do that stuff."

"What are your talking about?" she asks.

"The coke. Please don't do that to yourself. It's bad

enough with the booze. Don't do drugs. God, please don't do them, too."

"Oh, Simone." She leans her head back on the sofa cushion. "You don't understand," she says. "I'm so alone."

"You're *not* so alone. You have me and Father, and all your servants. There's always somebody here."

She looks at me and smiles sadly. "I am alone at a party. I am alone in a crowd. There is no one in here with me." She taps her head. She is right. I don't understand.

"Your father isn't here." She waves her arm around the room. "He won't do anything with me." She sits up suddenly and looks at me. "Don't you know any guys at school who are real jerks?"

"I go to an all-girls school, Mother."

"Yes, but you must see some guys around who are just so square, so dull. Don't you? They don't want to try anything. Don't want to get off their fat asses. Don't want to have any fun. Don't you know any guys like that?"

"I guess so."

"That's what your father's like. No fun at all. He used to be fun. More fun than any man I knew. Now, I don't know." She leans her head back again, and tears begin streaming down the side of her face into her hair, but she isn't really crying. "I need a drink," she whispers.

"Oh, God, Mother, no. You've had enough today. Please."

"Then go upstairs so I can do a line in peace."

Now I am crying.

"Stop it," she yells. "You're just like your father. A wimp. A drudge. Don't you have any sense of spirit, of fun, of what the hell, I want to live?"

"Of course I do. I just hate it when you—"

"Tell you what. I know what we can do." She gets up suddenly and begins rummaging through her drawers. I know what she is getting. I've been through this before. I've always said no. But tonight, maybe tonight if I say yes, she'll go to bed and not do the coke. "I have some really good stuff here," she says quietly. "Come on, Simone. You'll like this. Be with me. Let me split this with you. Then maybe I can sleep."

She sits next to me with her little box. She takes out a rolled joint, white and crinkled, like an evil little animal. She attachs a silver clip to it, holds it to her lips, and lights it. Inhales deeply, and speaks without breathing. "Here, sweetheart. Try it."

The clip switches hands. It's in mine. I put the skinny tip to my lips. It is wet from her lips. I take a deep drag, hold it, and hand the joint back to her.

"Oh, sweetheart," she says, her eyes shining and bright. "You're a real honey. You are. You are." A veil comes over her eyes and she drags again and hands it back to me. It goes on like that. She turns out the light and the glowing tip travels back and forth between us. She is perfectly silent. Nothing is happening to me. I drag deeper and longer, but nothing happens. I can't join her at all. I leave her alone even in this. She is quiet and soft, and I should feel safe with her near this way, but I can feel someone in the doorway. When I look, no one is there, but I am becoming more and more certain, until at last Mother says she is ready for bed now. She holds my face between her hands and rubs her cheeks on each of mine, twice, like a Russian diplomat's kiss, I think. Maybe there are Russians in the doorway.

Nothing is happening to me. She floats past in front of me to leave the room. Her aura stays behind, wisps of light from her nightgown, or is it the flower smell? I cannot move. Someone is in the doorway. She doesn't speak to whoever is there, but just floats past and up the stairs. Whoever it is begins to move into the room. I cannot look. I stare into the empty fireplace. I wait till the skin prickles on my arms and the hair stands up on the back of my neck. Perspiration drips down my sides and down the insides of my arms, and then I know who it is. It is Adilia.

But why am I so afraid? Maybe because Adilia is dead. Not just dead, but torn, I had heard the servants say that day. Crabs had eaten her face. "How can they be sure it is Adilia," I had asked, "without a face?" The kitchen help had grown quiet when they saw me there that afternoon.

I look up and over my shoulder. If I must see her eaten face, I will see it now. But no one is there.

I sink lower into the cushions of the sofa, draw my knees up to my face, and wrap my arms around my legs.

I bite my knees and shudder. Any minute I will see her, her chocolate arms, her laughing eyes, if the crabs left them.

I will never forget that last night with her, coming home on the ferry. We had shopped in town for hours, it seemed, buying fresh vegetables and fruit, and two large fish. Adilia carried them in netlike bags she had brought with her from Jamaica. We had started home, but she met a friend on the road, a black-skinned man who she said was from her hometown, and we had gone back to his rooms behind a colonial hotel where he worked, and he and Adilia had talked and laughed so loud. Once she had laughed so hard that she started to cry. And the man had held her shiny wet face to his chest until she stopped. I couldn't understand their language, yet I listened intently. Sometimes, I think, she talked about me. Her voice would get very low, and she would reach out and stroke my head as I sat there on the floor, playing with the man's dominoes.

That night the ferry was waiting at the dock with hardly any cars or people on it. It was slow to leave. It was already nine o'clock and dark. I was afraid of having to walk home from the pier. The chauffeur would be gone for the night, and it was all Adilia's fault for talking to her friend for so long. I was tired and angry with her. And she wouldn't carry me.

"Put your bag on your head and carry me," I had demanded.

But Adilia was distracted, far away. Her fingers draped

limply over my shoulder as she stared out into the blackest water.

"You are too big for that, chile. I tell you, Adilia cannot carry so much."

"On your head!" I yelled at her. "Put the bag on your head and lift me."

"Oh, Simone," she said. "You are working my nerves."

I can still feel the way I scowled at her, backed away from her gentle warm hands and crossed my arms. "You cannot do anything," I taunted. "You are stupid. You cannot be on time, you cannot carry packages on your head anymore. You can't walk on the water either. And you promised," I said, glaring at the shell bracelet on her wrist.

"I can," she said simply.

"No, you can't."

Her red cotton dress danced on her in the breeze. The package of fish and vegetables was by her feet at the railing, and her feet were wide and flat in her leather sandals, etched with black lines. "I think of my people," she said quietly. "I think of the sands of my country, and I am with God and I can do anything."

"No, you can't."

"Simone, I can."

"Then do it."

To reach back now and secure my hand in hers, to wrap my arms around her broad middle, to bury my face in the deep creases of her neck. But I stood there, my arms crossed, my skinny chest pressed hard against the ferry railing.

The ferry pulled away from the dock on the village side then. Like an ice cube slipping across the table we eased out into the troubled night. The engines vibrated under my feet. The dim light shone from the ferry poles, making the sky even darker, even harder to see, but the water was clear and distinct over the edge. It tumbled and churned, its sudsy foam glowing where there was no moon.

Adilia slipped her sandals off without bending. "I think of my people, my country, my Savior, and I am free," I heard her say. She began to hum then. A slow hymn that could lift the worst sinner off his feet and carry him over mountains.

She was going to do it! She was going to keep her promise! Adilia put one foot in the first rung of the railing and hoisted her other leg over the side. All the while humming. I uncrossed my arms and gripped the railing. I was smiling. My tiredness and grumpiness had left me, as I looked at Adilia poised there on the edge of the ferry, humming so to vibrate my very heart.

"My people, my country, my Savior," she said, and like stepping onto an escalator in a big department store, she stepped out.

I fully expected Adilia to walk out a ways, turn around and wave, bend down and throw up an armload of dark glowing water into the sky, and then come back to me. But Adilia sank like a stone. Out of sight. Sooner than I had thought. Deeper than anyone would have guessed.

They didn't find Adilia's body for three days, not until it washed up on the docks in the village where her countryman had lived, not until the crabs had had their way with her.

And now I wait for Adilia. I feel her in the room, come to scold me for making her walk on the water that night. Come to scold me with her crab-eaten face. But no one is here. There is only me, and the crabs on the cushions. The crabs that skitter out of sight when I look at them. But I know what they want. They want my eyes. Adilia's were so good and now they want mine. If I sit very still, they will not see me. If I keep my eyes closed tight over their knives, I won't see them.

Ali

There is nothing like a rich party, believe me. I mean fresh flowers everywhere, live music, vegetable platters shaped like baskets of flowers, where you pull the petals off and dip them in creamy thick ambrosia, and real live peacocks on the lawn. Peacocks! On the lawn!

Mom had agreed to let me go, I think mostly to keep "that poor girl Simone company." That's how she'd begun to refer to the princess of Dune Island after our lunch—that poor girl.

Ma—peacocks!

But whatever her reason, I was grateful. I was treated to a new summer dress of white flimsy Indian cotton that swished around my calves and showed off my new tan. And earlier that afternoon, Simone had French braided my hair. That girl . . . I couldn't believe her. Here she had told Brendan and Sammy that sure she would go water-skiing, just check it out with Ali, and she left me holding the bag. What a jerk I must have looked like. I hadn't really prepared what I'd say if it came up, so when Sammy called I had to think fast. I said I'd twisted my shoulder, that I'd dislocated it once before and I had to be careful. Maybe some other time. Shades of skiing in Switzerland and never walking again, right? I hated myself. But as Simone slowly brushed out my hair, she reassured me that sacred oaths were more important than telling little untruths, and the party that night would be her chance to make it up to me.

We'd see.

The sky was a beautiful sunset pink as the four of us sat stiffly in the white gazebo, which rose up a little higher than the yard around it. From inside it we could see the lawns, the large house with warm yellow lights beginning to glow in the windows, the people arriving in long cars, surrendering them to hired island men who took the cars and parked them carefully out of sight. And the bay. I swear it was like a calendar shot, simply perfect, and I was sure then it was all the wealth that made it look so good. I knew it didn't look the same from the cottage.

The water was changing colors as I watched, the trees on the opposite shore were growing darker, and the last birds of the day flew past in silhouettes as if they'd been hired to add to the spectacle.

And Brendan. Brendan. He was all in white, white jeans, white boat shoes, and a white cotton shirt with the sleeves rolled up just right, and the neck opened just right, and a white tie loosened and drooping around his neck. Just right. His hair curled softly around his neck, and when he walked past me I got a whiff of something wonderful. A cologne or soap that reminded me of a new pink doll from my past. Ah, Brendan.

Sammy looked nice, but a little stiff in his faded madras shirt and his dark jeans. His black knit tie was tight around his neck, and he kept sticking his finger into his collar. "My father says he had to wear one of these to school every day. Can you imagine? Who invented this torture?"

"Oh, take it off," said Simone, brazenly walking right up to him and loosening it. If you had told me what Simone was going to wear that night, I would have said, Never! So tacky! I mean lavender pajamas and silver sandals? How else could I describe them? But that's what they were. On me, it would have looked like a Halloween costume. On Simone, it looked like an ingenious illusion. Yards and yards of thin silver chains hugged her hips and waist, and her hair hung down her back like a dark shining mane. And she moved like a lioness. "On second thought," she said to Sammy, "you might want to loosen it, but keep it on in case we play strip Ping-Pong later."

"Strip Ping-Pong?" they both said in unison.

I laughed. "Simone! I never heard of such a thing."

"Sure." She smiled. "You play doubles, and whoever misses has to take off an article of clothing. So keep your tie on, Sammy."

"Right," I said. "Easy for you. You have seventy chain belts on." I looked at Brendan, and he was leaning there against the low wall of the gazebo grinning at Simone. I watched him.

"But *I'm* a champion Ping-Pong player," he taunted. "I've got a trophy to prove it."

"No proof by me," Simone teased. I glared at her. First I have to lie for her, and then this?

"Simone," I said. "Why don't we get a tray of those vegetable flowers to bring up here?"

"And beers?" she asked. "You two want beer?"

They nodded, and I followed Simone out of the gazebo and across the lawn. "What are you doing?" I muttered to her.

She looked at me startled. "What do you mean?"

"You know what I mean. Why are you flirting with Brendan? Strip Ping-Pong, my ass! What are you *doing*?"

She stopped and glared at me. "I am not flirting with Brendan. If you want to know the truth, I was trying to flirt with Sammy in hopes that you'd make some kind of move, but you just sit there like a lump. What do you want me to do? Put Brendan in your lap for you?"

She turned and continued across the lawn. I kept up with her. Silent. What was I doing? Just because she was pretty and threatening and just because Brendan was smiling at her? She was right. I wasn't really doing anything myself. I didn't even know what to do.

"So what do I do?" I asked.

"Be yourself," she said, glancing back at me. "Only more."

"Only more," I muttered, and followed her in the back door of the house, the servants' entry to the back pantry near the kitchen. The screen door flung open, we both barged right in, and there was Mrs. Silver, head thrown back, hoisting a bottle of wine to her mouth. Simone froze.

"Mother!"

"Simone, darling." Mrs. Silver wiped the backs of her fingers across her lips. She looked ashamed. "I was just . . . ah, here, taste this, dear. It's been here so long, and I didn't want to serve it unless it's just right. You know, only the best at the Silvers' party."

She held out the bottle to Simone, who pushed it aside and walked past her. Simone went to the refrigerator, and took two beers and two Cokes. She slammed them down angrily onto a tray with fresh vegetables and dip.

"Here, Ali," Mrs. Silver said holding the bottle out to me. "This hasn't gotten bad, do you think?"

I put my nose to the top of the bottle for her and sniffed. "You couldn't tell by me, Mrs. Silver."

"Oh, dear, I'll just have to ask your father," she said. She left the room hurriedly. Simone and I looked at each other. Then she looked away and tried to rearrange the cans on the tray.

"Help me with this," she ordered.

I took the drinks from her, and we both knew she was trembling. "And when it gets dark," she said, "we'll go downstairs and play Ping-Pong and our own music."

"Not strip," I said.

"Of course not," she said in a funny make-believe accent, abruptly light and silly. "Don't be ridiculous," and I followed her out the door.

The basement was not the kind I was used to—no cinderblock walls painted yellow, buckled linoleum, head-smacking pipes in the ceiling. This basement was—well, it's wasn't a basement, or a cellar, or even a family room. It was just a *downstairs*. Oak-paneled walls, red carpeting, recessed lighting, a fireplace, and besides the Ping-Pong table at one end, there was a pool table at the other and a chandelier above it like something out of the wild west.

First we played pool. Simone was good at it, but I had never played before, so Brendan showed me how, cupping his hand over mine, leaning me over the edge, teaching me how to aim. I can still see his face, so close, one eye squinched up, his cheek tight and crinkled along his eye. We ate raw vegetables like crazy, the four of us, laughing and taking shots, dumping each other's balls, setting up, twisting the cues in chalk. I was just getting the hang of it when Sammy suggested Ping-Pong.

"Strip Ping-Pong?" Brendan asked, grinning at Simone. I looked at her quick, but she wasn't even looking at Brendan. She was flipping her hair over her shoulder.

"I know," Sammy said, maybe as anxious as I was not to play strip Ping-Pong. "Let's play elimination Ping-Pong."

"Do we eliminate clothes?" Brendan persisted, reaching

out and slipping a finger into one of Simone's chains. She slapped his hand playfully.

"No," Sammy answered. "Look, I'll show you." He went over to the Ping-Pong table and picked up a paddle. "Come on."

We joined him as if for doubles, me and Brendan on one end, Simone on the other with Sammy. Gently we began to paddle the hard hollow ball back and forth until it worked up a nice easy rhythm. We were pretty good, well matched, although I had the feeling that the guys were holding back a bit.

"All right now," Sammy said, catching the ball in his hand. "Now we play with only one paddle on a side." He dropped his paddle under the table and put Simone's on the center line. Brendan and I did the same.

"Sammy missed his calling," Brendan whispered to me. "He's a frustrated camp counselor, dying to break out."

"I heard that!" Sammy laughed. "Okay now, children, listen up. Volley the ball back and forth nice and easy. You hit the ball and then put the paddle quickly on the line here so that your partner is ready for the next volley. Got it?"

He served to Brendan, who hit it and put his paddle on the table. Meanwhile Sammy had placed his paddle on the line and Simone picked it up and volleyed back. I panicked, picked the paddle up too late and swatted at the ball with my other hand.

"No hands, Ali-cat," Sammy said, as if I didn't know.

"Now he tells me," I said.

I served the ball and we all volleyed back and forth. We got a consistent rhythm going again, and picking up the paddle and putting it down added a sort of frenzied tension, until we were all laughing. We were good partners, Brendan and me. We were working up a championship pace together.

"All right," Sammy announced, scooping the ball from the air with his hand once again. "You are now ready for elimination Ping-Pong. The big time! This is it!"

Simone was flushed and pretty. She had a way of watching Sammy when he talked that bordered on adoration. It was amazing to watch. I was even beginning to wonder if she was growing to like Sammy, when she suddenly turned her eyes on Brendan with the same exact expression. She glowed, flashed her even teeth at him, and turned back to Sammy. I didn't get it.

"What you do is," Sammy was saying, "it's still only one paddle to a side, but this time when you hit the ball, not only do you place the paddle on the table, but you also run to the other side. The next person on the other side will hit the ball back, put down the paddle, and run to your side. Got it? And what happens is, we're all running around the table, hit and run, hit and run."

"What?" we all groaned. "That's crazy!"

"Come on," he coaxed. "Try it."

He served the ball and ran to our side of the table. Brendan hit it back and ran to Simone's side. She hit it and ran to our side. I hit it back and ran to Brendan's. It was hysterical. We were all four of us running in a big circle around the Ping-Pong table, each stopping at the ends to pick up the paddle, hit the ball, lay it down, and run. The antics and the silliness were almost unbearable. My cheeks soon ached from the laughing.

Simone finally missed the ball and went after it beneath the pool table.

"But why do you call it elimination Ping-Pong?" she asked.

"Well," Sammy answered coolly, "I'll show you. See how you missed the ball? Well, if we were playing a real game, that would eliminate you. And then there'd only be three players left. Kind of like musical chairs."

"That's impossible," Brendan said.

"Difficult, yes, but not impossible," Sammy said. "Because then when the next person misses, he or she is eliminated, and then there are only two left."

"Still running around the table?" I asked.

Sammy nodded. "I must warn you. I'm the champion elimination player at my rec center. I can play Ping-Pong . . . alone."

"You're crazy," Brendan said.

Sammy smiled. "Let's do it," he said. "Are you ready?"

We all looked at each other doubtfully. Sammy was beaming. "Okay," he said, poised to serve. "Ready to go?"

"Ready!" we shouted. Brendan was crouched beside me ready to run. I started to laugh.

Sammy served and ran, Brendan hit it back and ran, Simone, then me. We trotted at a nice easy pace around the table, following each other after each hit. We each picked up our own pace based on the rhythm of the one before us. We were no longer partners but on our own, and more than trying to defeat each other there was a challenge in keeping up the game, keeping the ball going. Until Simone missed.

"Elimination," Sammy said. He was concentrating hard. "Okay, Simone. Back off now. It's just the three of us left. Are you ready, gang?"

Brendan and I nodded.

"You guys serve," Sammy said, tossing the ball to me.

I served to Sammy, and ran, Sammy hit it back, and ran, Brendan hit it and I had to be there quick to hit it back. With just three of us we had to run faster, think sharper. The pace was different, tenser, but we went on and on, not laughing now, but serious, intent. The only sound was our muffled footsteps on the thick carpeting and the delicate sound of the ball hitting back and forth. Round and round we went, locked in our attention on the little ball, locked in a dance with each other, Brendan, Sammy, and me. Until Brendan missed.

"Elimination," Sammy said again. He was looking at me intently. "All right, Ali, it's between you and me now."

"This is impossible," Brendan scoffed. "You can't do this with only two of you."

Sammy nodded at me. Stared at me. "We can do it. I've done it. You serve, Ali-cat."

I nodded back.

"Run faster," he told me, "but hit slower, okay?"

"Okay." I served the ball gently to Sammy and ran to his side of the table. He hit it gently back and I realized he had to run quickly alongside the ball to the end and hit it again. He was the only one there now. I hit it gently and realized I would have to tear around to the end of the table myself. I just made it, throwing myself across the table and barely hitting it. Sammy hit it back, and ran alongside it. He was calmer. I was like a maniac, throwing myself across the table to make it each time. I was screaming with laughter inside, but locked in concentration on the outside. I don't think I had ever been so focused in on anything in my life. It was so hard, but so possible. We actually worked up a syncopated lopsided rhythm that worked in a sort of frenzied way, until I missed.

"What a game," I laughed. "I have never played Ping-Pong like that."

"It's not over," Sammy said, poising himself to serve.

"You're going to do this alone?" I asked, unbelieving, out of breath.

"Watch me," he said.

He served then, an easy soft lob that went high and bounced to the other side of the table. He was there by the time it came down, hit it another high lob and ran like mad around the other side, hit it again, over and over. I had never seen anything like it. Here was Sammy playing Ping-Pong by himself. Until he missed. We dissolved into laughter, shook hands like victors, hugged like teammates, and looked around.

Brendan and Simone were gone.

"Where'd everybody go?" he asked.

I shrugged, looked around. "Maybe for beer or soda, you think?"

But I knew. I'd known all along, hadn't I?

I guess Sammy knew, too. "That, Brendan," he sighed. "Well, how about a game of darts while we wait to see if they come back?"

"Sure," I said. "Why not?"

And we played darts for about a half an hour and they never did come back. Sammy and I grew quiet with each other. And I was growing sadder and sadder. Sammy must have felt it. Finally he pulled the blue-and-red darts out of the board and looked at me. "What do you say? Want me to walk you home?"

"Yeah. It's getting late."

We slipped out the back door of the kitchen, avoiding all the guests who were still there, their voices and the live music filling the summer air. We walked silently across the dark lawn, lightning bugs flickering low and slow. "How will you get home?" I asked.

"I'll walk," Sammy said. "It's a nice night."

"Want my father to drive you?"

"Nah. I like walking."

"Mmm. Me, too."

"You're a pretty good Ping-Pong player," Sammy said.

The lit cottage was before us like a stupid grinning pumpkin on a hill. I smiled sadly. "You're just looking for compliments," I said. "I've never seen anybody as good as you."

"True, true," he teased. "Took years of practice, though. Nothing comes easy, you know."

Smart Sammy. Nothing comes easy. "That's for sure," I agreed. He probably hadn't the slightest idea what I was really talking about. But by that time we were at the cottage.

"I'll give you a call soon," Sammy said. "And maybe when that shoulder is better, we can go water-skiing."

"Sure," I told him. "It's a lot better already."

Simone

No one is left. There are glasses here and there on the lawn, an empty tray down near the water, and the ridiculous peacocks are caged by the gazebo. In the morning Larsen will come and rake up the flattened grass and do any repairs. But now it looks deserted, abandoned, like maybe a bomb fell and everyone disintegrated on the spot. Here by this sweater I can imagine a little pile of dust, a woman trapped mid sentence by the bomb. *Psst.* Snuffed out like a candle in the rain. Here stood the band. On the upbeat, *boom*, they're granulated. Everyone is vaporized, except for me. Simone Silver, the princess of Dune Island.

I wonder if I look different now. I had listened to the sound of Brendan's car driving off into the distance. Long after it's gone, I still listen for it. My hair is full of sand. It's in my teeth, inside my clothes, in my eyes. But I don't care. It was worth it, I guess. I try to keep the image of his face in my mind, but it escapes me. All I remember are his hands when he quickly unbuttoned his glowing white shirt against the dark sky and tossed it aside. That's all that's really clear.

I can tell I won't be able to sleep tonight . . . or this morning, whatever this is. I have a buzz in my ears that keeps me alert. It's as if I have lost the shutdown valve, the off switch that will let in sleep. The back door is locked. Father has locked up without even checking to see if I was in. Anger begins to well up inside me, until I remind myself what I've done. Then I smile, like a cat, like a temptress. I try the sliding glass doors on the living room, and one slides silently under the pressure of my hand. I hope Mother is not on the sofa. Or on the floor. What would it matter? I don't know. I don't know. I just don't want to look at her face. I want Brendan's to be the last face I've seen. I won't look at anyone again. Not till he comes back. If he comes back.

The living room is dark and cleaned up already. The piano is wiped, the glasses are gone. Just the carpet—I feel it crunchy in spots under my bare feet as I tiptoe across the room. Then up the steps. Not a sound. No one has missed me. Did they think I was tucked in tight, sound asleep? No, they couldn't have thought that. My bedroom door is open. My bed is smooth. They didn't even look.

I step inside my room and slam the door as hard as I can. I feel the blood pounding in my head. There is no one to talk to. No one who cares. If only Adilia were still alive. She would understand. And listen to me. I would visit her in the cottage, put my head in her lap, and tell her all about Brendan, about what we'd done, and she wouldn't scold me, wouldn't judge. She'd smooth my hair and ask what the moon had been like and if his breath had tasted like butter creams.

I ache for her. Like that one instant I had ached for Brendan before he came to me. Not in my body like it was for him, but in my heart, in the roof of my mouth, in my eyes. I pick up the phone. I could call the cottage. How many times have I done that, dialed the number at the cottage, knowing no one was there, but knowing the phone was ringing in a place that once held Adilia? We never had a phone there till years after she was gone. She wouldn't have liked it anyway. She liked faces and touching while she talked.

I remember that night once when she was visiting her sister in the city. Mother had fixed my bath. Drawn the water, tossed me a washcloth and soap, and told me to wash. No big dark hands rubbing me down, tickling me, making me laugh. And when I came out of the tub, I was still dirty, rivers of play running down the inside of my arms, and I don't remember how it happened, but Mother had pushed me, pushed me and yelled and my feet were wet and the marble floor was slippery, and like a watermelon pit squirting from between tight lips, I had shot across the floor and hit my head on the pedestal sink before I went down.

Father had held me and patted me, *The Wall Street Journal* spread out on my bed, but I wouldn't be comforted. I tormented them, wailing, "A-DEEL-ya! A-DEEL-ya!" over and over, until finally he dialed her number in the city for me, and held me wrapped in a thick towel on his lap.

"Adilia?" I whispered. "When are you coming back?"

"Tomorrow, chile. I told you that, now, didn't I? What is the matter with you?"

"I'm in trouble," I said, looking down at my arms, streaked with summer dirt.

I listened to her laughter over the phone. "Oh, my nerves, chile. I'll be back. You go to sleep now. Listen to the ferry horn. See if it calls your name tonight."

"Good night, Adilia," I said, pushing the phone back to Father. I rolled off his lap onto my bed and wouldn't let anyone touch me again. I didn't want to hear another voice until it was Adilia's, didn't want to see another face, feel another touch. I listened for the ferry horn all night long and slept in the thick towel.

The ferry horn calls me now. The phone is waiting and the cottage is not empty. But I have to talk to someone. I'll call the cottage. Maybe they are sleeping soundly. Maybe it will just ring and ring. If Charles A. Mintz answers, I'll hang up. If Ali answers . . . maybe she'll talk to me. Maybe she'll understand, and I can tell her.

I dial the number. It rings only twice.

"Hello?" A groggy Ali.

"It's Simone, Ali. Can you talk?"

She coughs. I hear rustlings. "*Can* I talk? Don't you mean *will* I talk?"

Easy, Simone, go slow. "Will you talk to me?"

"Why? Why are you even calling me?"

"You're my friend. My only friend. Remember, I told you?"

"But why are you calling me. Want to go water-skiing, huh? Shall we make plans for tomorrow? With the boys?"

We are silent. Her anger hangs in the air like bats. For long moments. Maybe for five minutes. We don't say a word. Then I tell her. "I'm not a virgin anymore."

"Sorry to hear it."

But she doesn't hang up.

"I have to talk to somebody, Ali. Can't I talk to you?"

"Great choice, Simone. I'm probably the best person in the world for you to talk to about that. And I can't imagine who it was. Let me guess. Could it have been Brendan?"

"Yes."

"Funny thing about that, Simone, but weren't you supposed to be my friend? Weren't you supposed to help me out with this? Didn't we string up some damned bracelets about this very thing? You're full of it, you know that?"

"You would have done the same thing, Ali. You know you would have. It was me he wanted to be with. If he had wanted to be with you, he would have been with you."

"Yeah, but one thing, Simone. You knew I liked him. Didn't that count for something? Would you rip off my pocketbook, too, if you liked it? Would you steal my earrings?"

"You don't own Brendan."

Ali is quiet. "You're right. But what about the oaths? Huh? What about them?"

"I'm not good at promises. They're hard for me."

Ali snorts.

And again a long, dull silence. I think maybe she's fallen asleep, and then she asks, "Well, was he good?"

"Yes. I guess so."

"You guess so? Was he gentle?"

"Yes. Gentle. Strong."

Ali sighs a long, sad sigh. "Listen," she says, "I can't do this. If you have to talk, call information. Or some loss-of-virginity hotline. I just can't handle this." And she hangs up. Leaves me with the emptiness and no one else to call. I feel as if I've just gotten married, and no one came, no one cared, not even the groom.

Ali

I thought of leaving right then. And in the morning at breakfast, I thought of it again. After all, Mom was pretty lonely back home all by herself, and Daddy was really into his book. He was near the end, he said, and was beginning to look right through me and spout dialogue that had nothing to do with where we were at all. Like I'd said—

"Daddy, would you pass the sugar?"

He had answered, "That's what he always did," and passed the sugar. He looked at me. "But she should have known. Surely she had known all along. But if not. She would know soon."

Daddy thought he could write and be a person at the same time. Like folding laundry and holding a conversation. It didn't work with him.

"Earth calling Charlie Mintz," I said. "Earth calling Charlie Mintz. Are you there?"

His glassy stare slowly came into focus. I could imagine being in his head and suddenly seeing the world change before him magically from the characters in his book, to me, his daughter, Alison Mintz, in full color, Dolby sound, live.

He stared at me. I glared at him. "What's the matter?" he asked. I could tell he was really with me now.

"You're so out of it. So gone," I complained.

"You're right," he said. "You're absolutely right. But what's the problem? You agreed to live with this spaced-out martian this summer. No problem, you said, remember? You knew I wasn't an entertainment committee."

"Yeah, but even Lois is more company than—"

"Ali," he said threateningly, slowly. "You knew what the deal was."

I shut up and grew sulky inside. What good would he be to talk to anyway? He wouldn't understand anything about Simone. Or Brendan. We were quiet for a while, just eating our cereal and sipping coffee. I thought he'd retreated back into his fiction fantasy when suddenly he asked, "So how was your party last night?"

"Peacocks," I answered.

"Peacocks?"

"They had live peacocks on the lawn. Do you believe it?"

"Flannery O'Connor raised peacocks. You know, Ali, you might be ready for some of her stories."

I left the table and dumped my cereal dish in the sink. How did it always get back to books and stories and writing? I was ready to dump his cereal on his head. He didn't care about me, or the party. Just his books.

"But that's beside the point, isn't it?" he asked. What was he, a mind reader? "Tell me about the party."

"It stunk." I rinsed out the bowl. Now I didn't want to talk.

"You sweet on that Sammy kid?" he asked.

"No," I answered, glaring at him. "I'm not sweet on anybody."

"Sounds like a woman scorned," he teased. Exactly what I didn't need. The wet cereal bowl slipped from my hand and crashed onto the floor, sending Lois flying into the next room. Angrily I began throwing the broken pieces into the garbage. Tears welled into my eyes and I began to sob.

"Oh, just leave me alone, would you?" I shouted. "Go back to your tomb." I jammed the rest of the pieces in the garbage and slammed out the screen door. I collapsed on the back steps and put my head on my knees and cried. Cried for my embarrassment. My losses. My spacy father. I heard the door open behind me and close quietly. He sat down beside me on the step.

"Can I get you something, Pepper?" he asked gently. "A guru? A doctor? A fairy godmother, maybe?"

I wiped the tears off my face with the palms of my hands. I was a mess. I looked at him, then away. "Fairy godmother," I answered.

He smiled at me, and I put my head on his shoulder as his arm went around me, "What's up?" he asked.

"Are you here?" I asked, turning to look into his eyes carefully. "Really here?"

He nodded, and I put my head back on his shoulder.

"I'm just embarrassed I guess. I had this stupid crush on that guy Brendan, really liked him, and I thought maybe he might like me, but it turned out he and Simone went off last night. She's so pretty, Daddy, so rich, so perfect. I hate her."

"Ah," he said softly. "I know I'm your father, Pepper, and that probably doesn't count for much, but I know a good-looking woman when I see one. And Simone Silver is pretty, but so are you." He examined my face. "Different, but still pretty." He wiped my face with the side of his hand. "How can I explain it? Like which is prettier, a rose or a daisy?"

"Roses cost more," I said.

"Money. Cost. Rich," he moaned. "That doesn't count for anything. You know what my favorite flower is? That purple stuff that grows along the parkway in the summer. I don't even know what it is, but I think that purple haze is the most beautiful sight when I'm riding along."

"You have great taste," I teased. "Is that what I'm like? Weeds on the highway?"

"Maybe," he answered.

"But even pretty aside, Daddy, she was my friend. She knew I liked Brendan. She knew it, and what does she do? She takes off with him."

"What'd they do, go to Reno or something?"

"No, they had sex."

"Oh."

Dead silence. Maybe I shouldn't have said that.

"But didn't they just meet each other?" he asked.

"Yeah. Pretty much, I guess."

"That's not how you want it to be for you, Ali." He looked at me. "Is it?"

"No, I guess not. It's not that I wanted *sex*. I wanted him to like me, that's all. And I wanted a wild summer romance, you know?"

We both laughed. I sounded silly even to myself. "But no sex," he said. My eyes were still crying, and my face sort of ached from going so quick from tears to laughter. "Promise me, Alison, my baby, promise me you'll never have sex." He was laughing and shaking me by the shoulders. God, I loved him.

We grew quiet and I dropped my head on his shoulder again. "Whew," he whispered. "Where's your mother when I need her?"

"You're doing fine," I told him.

"So are you," he said.

"Think I should go back home? Think Mom needs me?"

"That's not the best reason to go back home," he said.

"I know. But I don't want to hang out with Simone anymore. I don't trust her. And I just don't know what else to do here. At home I could probably get into a painting workshop at the high school, or Chinese cooking or something." I noticed I still had the shell bracelet on. I slipped it off my wrist and weighed it in my palm.

"Tell you what," he offered. "Sit on it a bit. Don't make any decision right now while you're upset. Why don't you mull it around, and go to Harborville with me tonight again? And tomorrow we'll talk about it and see what we come up with."

"Okay. Meanwhile, maybe I'll clean up the kitchen really good while you go back to work. Organize the cabinets or something."

He stared at me. "So it's come to this, has it?"

It had.

We were a little bit late getting to Daddy's meeting that night. He'd been relieved of coffee-making and was now cleanup, which meant we'd be the last to leave instead of the first to arrive. There were speakers from the city, and it was somebody's anniversary, so there were bright tablecloths on the tables and a sugary layer cake. Everyone was in a party mood, happy and laughing. A couple of the women who remembered me said hello and hooked me into serving the cake with them.

The meeting began, and as the first speaker started, we each took a tray filled with slices of cake impaled with plastic forks on paper plates, and made our way up and down the tables offering them to anyone who wanted a piece. I went up the side of the room where there were people sitting along the wall. I made my way along till I was at the front door and my tray was empty. I was just about to head back to the kitchen when I stopped in my tracks.

A man stumbled into the doorway and stood looking into the room. I backed up but couldn't take my eyes off him. It was obvious that he was very drunk. *Sick,* Daddy would say. The man had thrown up all over his shirt. There was a smirk on his face.

And it was Frank.

I didn't know what to do. Here was Frank, Sammy and Brendan's friend and co-worker, and all I could feel was fear. I didn't want him to recognize me, to look at me. My stomach turned as his smell wafted into the room. But before I could turn and run to the kitchen, two men appeared from behind me, and in a flash, they escorted Frank back out the door to the men's room.

I dumped the tray in the kitchen and went out to sit by Daddy. It seemed Frank's entrance hadn't been noticed. The meeting went on, the speaker kept talking, and the people were laughing.

"What's wrong?" Daddy asked, leaning toward me and whispering.

"Did you see that man?" I asked.

"Yes. Frank."

"That's the guy who works with Sammy and Brendan at the Pridley. I thought he had his ninety days."

"He did," Daddy whispered. "He's having a hard time of it. Keeps drifting in and out."

"Why?" I searched Daddy's eyes. Why would someone pick up a drink again after ninety days? Would my father after fifteen years?

Daddy shrugged. "Some people don't follow suggestions," he told me. "Makes it hard."

"Suggestions like what?"

"Oh, like make a lot of meetings. Get honest. Don't go into the lion's den."

The lion's den. I remembered Frank talking about the lion's den—the parties at the Silvers'. I couldn't remember seeing Frank there at the party the night before, but then we hadn't really been in the mainstream of the party the whole night. I wondered if Sammy and Brendan would have mentioned that Frank was there. But there were lots of other lion's dens in this world.

Daddy motioned his head to the door. Frank and the two men were coming down the steps carefully. Frank had washed up a bit and was down to just his T-shirt. With hands on his shoulders they led him to the other side of the room and sat him down. He sat there quietly the rest of the night, grinning, swaying, and holding a trembling cup of coffee to his lips once in a while. I didn't speak to him this time. I doubt he saw me.

It was beginning to drizzle as Daddy and I reached the ferry home, but we got out of the car anyway. The black water had a rough dappled texture, and the sky had a pale glow.

"Still haven't found that book of yours," the ferryman said, cloaked in his yellow rubber cape. He took our tickets, and I glanced at Daddy. He was perfectly serious.

"Might have gone out of print by now," he answered. I hid my smile.

Suddenly the ferry lurched a bit and the ferryman caught his balance. "Currents are rough tonight," he told us. "Full moon, high tides. You'd never guess what the bay's like down there under the surface. It's a regular underground tornado."

"Anybody ever drown out here?" I asked, suddenly remembering Simone's story, wondering if it were true or just another of her tales.

"Been some," he answered. "Not when I've been aboard, thank goodness, but yeah, there've been a few drownings. Quite a while ago." In the green light of the ferry lamp I saw a smile spread over his face. "There was one," he began like a teller of ghost stories, "a great big fat Jamaican woman." He laughed. "You would've thought she'd float, that one."

I stared at him. "That's funny?" I felt Daddy's shoulder nudge mine a bit.

"Well, no. I guess not. No. Not at all. It's just that if you'd seen her—"

I stared at him and he squirmed.

"You're right," he admitted. "It wasn't funny. As a matter of fact, it was kind of sad, as I remember the way it was told. Seems she was with a little kid who saw the whole thing. Some little girl from one of the big estates. It was her nanny or something. Kid was pretty upset, they said."

I felt the ferry shift under my feet. Or was it a shift inside myself? I thought of Simone as a little child, standing here at this very railing. A shiver ran through me. When the ferryman moved on, Daddy looked at me. "What was all that about?" he asked.

"That was Simone's nanny," I said.

He was quiet, and then he said, "Well, I guess it's not all peacocks and pool filters, is it, Pepper?"

I guessed it wasn't.

Simone

It's been over a week since I've seen Brendan. I haven't left the house. "Will Brendan call today? Will he ever call me?" I ask this of the cards. "Today, yesterday, tomorrow, ago and to be." Only two are right side up. A probable no. My own card has appeared, and even it is upside down. My card. Adilia had dubbed me the Page of Swords—a willful, secretive child who could be unkind to get her way. Upside down the page of swords is malicious, an imposter.

I am not! I am not! I shout inside myself and fling the card across my room. I am not an imposter. I am not malicious. But Ali's face seems to watch me. None of this was worth it. Now I don't have Ali *or* Brendan. And I never really wanted him in the first place. I don't know why I did that—followed him that way up the stairs, away from the sound of the Ping-Pong ball, the laughter, through the dunes to the water. All the while watching myself as if from a distance, knowing I wouldn't like that girl there, that one on the beach, so easy, so agreeable. So deceitful.

Now I am alone again. I tell them I have a cold and they leave me alone. Only Ramona brings me trays of food, drifting into the room, scooping up pieces of laundry, towels. She is small. Her dark hair is shiny and straight, but she does the things Adilia once did—opening windows, wiping fingerprints with her apron. I am almost tempted to talk to her. What would I say? Ramona, I have been with a man. I am all alone. Ramona, the cards don't say what I need to hear.

"Can I ask the cards a question for you, Ramona?"

She is startled and looks at me, folding the towels over her arms. She hugs them to herself. "A question?"

"Yes. Ask me a question. Any question that needs a yes or no answer and I will tell you." I shuffle the tarot cards and hold the deck out to her, but she doesn't take them. She shakes her head.

"Why would I need to know? Any answers I need will come to me. In time."

"Not all answers," I coax. "Like, will your husband be true—"

"My husband is true," she says.

"Will you have a lot of money—"

"I will never have a lot of money."

She has all the answers. We stare at each other, and I whisper, "Will I ever learn to be a good friend?"

"You will learn," she tells me.

"Will I ever be loved?"

"In time," she says.

The cards fall heavily from my hand. "You don't need the cards, do you, Ramona?"

"Neither do you. Ask your heart for your answers."

"But the tarot cards are a road to my heart."

Ramona shrugs and glances around the room for more things. "I'm leaving now for the night," she says. "I'll do laundry first thing in the morning, so if there's anything you want done, I'll take it now."

"No, you've got it all," I say, beginning to wrap the cards up in the silk scarf. "Where's my mother?"

"In the den with a gentleman," she tells me. Without looking at me.

A gentleman? "And my father?"

"In the city." She rolls the clothes into a bundle and reaches for the doorknob. She looks back and smiles at me. "There's peach ice cream in the freezer. In case you're hungry later."

"Thanks, Ramona. See you tomorrow."

She closes the door silently, leaving such an emptiness in my room again. I suddenly feel as if I'm locked in a glass bubble. I hear the blood rushing through my head, past my ears, pounding, running. It's night and I'm not even tired because I have been in here all day. Away in my room with my records, and my synthetic nail mix. I feel like doing something. Something risky. Something dangerous. I begin to pace the room. I should exercise.

Maybe I will go ride my bike through the hills in the darkness.

I hear a car pull up outside and look out the window. It is Ramona's husband. Her faithful husband, who, along with her, will never be rich. How good it must feel to be so certain. Like being a train on a railroad track. Me, I am more like a hoofed animal in a rocky place. I watch from above as Ramona leaves from the side of the house, opens the car door, and slides in. I lift my window a minute, feeling the warm air gushing in, but I can't hear anything. What do they speak about? How does he sound? The car chugs in place for an instant and then begins its way out of the driveway. As it leaves, I see a car parked under the linden by the side of the drive. The black convertible. No one is inside it. Its radio is off. Fear prickles up the inside of my arms.

Whose car is that? Ramona said there was a gentleman with Mother. Slowly and methodically I begin to get dressed. I am going for a bike ride, I tell myself. But I know what I'm really doing. I pull on sweatpants and a T-shirt. I lace up my sneakers. I flip on my stereo so it sounds like I'm in my room, close the door gently, and start down the steps. It's quiet. No voices. No one is in the living room. Ramona said they were in the den. Silently I make my way across the living room to the glass doors. They slide when I touch them, and I slip out into the cricket-heavy darkness. Sticking close to the house, I make my way along the foundation, behind the shrubs, to the picture windows of the den.

A gull shrieks overhead and I panic, breathe deeply, and try to calm my shaking before I go any farther. I crouch down and creep the rest of the way. From the shadow of the shrubbery and the partial cover of a thin curtain, I look into the den. I taste salt, taste salt as I see my mother standing in the center of the den, in her soft nightgown, laughing, and her arms are around the neck of a man I do not know. He slips a canvas bag from his shoulder and places it gently on the table. I cannot hear what he says, but he turns back to my mother and they kiss. My mother. There is a glass in her hand, and she pushes him away to drink from it. I can tell she's very drunk. He walks to the bar and turns to speak to her. It's then that I recognize him. I *do* know this man. It's Brendan and Sammy's friend. The water-skier. Frank. My mother is with Frank.

I feel like I want to crash through the window, kill them both. I can imagine the dull expression on my mother's face, the deadness. Frank pours himself a drink and then turns to his bag on the table. It's been him all along. It's been Frank's car that I've seen. He's the one who's been bringing the coke to her. I watch as he unzips the bag and takes out a round bottle with a glass pipe, and sitting on the edge of the sofa, he begins to lay out his paraphernalia. My mother moves close and he's instructing her. He steadies the glass, it looks like he places something on the top, he lights the tip of a pencil, and she draws close to him, sits on his knee. How do I know this is dangerous? How do I know I must stop them, but the sight of her there, the sound of their laughter penetrating the plate-glass window, is more than I can bear. "Cook it up!" I hear my mother's voice. Cook it up, she says. And I am very frightened. I don't belong here. I don't belong anywhere.

Backing up away from the house, catching on the shrubs, but trying not to panic and bolt, I move as fast as I can. I have to get away from here. I can't stay here while this happens. I have to go. I run over the dark lawn to the carriage house. My bike is near the doorway and I roll it out. The headlight's battery is long dead. It's better. I'll be invisible. I'll disappear into the dark forest like a deer and never be seen again. I mount the bike and pedal heavily up the hill to the roadway. I pass close to the cottage to get to the road. I don't see anyone, but the lights are on inside and there's the muffled sound of music. If only Ali—

Then there is an explosion behind me that I feel in my ribs, in my lungs, and my bike wavers. I turn back to the house and I wonder for a minute why it looks so beautiful like that, with the den bright yellow and flickering. Flickering. The den is aglow with a pulsing light.

"What was that?" I hear someone call from the cottage behind me. I hear them running up to me. I don't look at them, but we stand there together, looking back at my house.

"Fire department!" someone shouts.

"How? What's happened? What is it?" I turn and Ali is beside me. Her father is running toward the cottage and she is staring at me. Funny, I had never noticed before how perfect her face is, how her nose is exactly centered in her face and how her eyes are perfectly round. Perfect round saucers, like dishes.

"Simone? Are you all right?"

Sammy is next to her. He reaches out and squeezes my shoulder. "What's happened?" His face is just like hers. I can barely tell them apart, two faces like masks in a costume store, staring at me, waiting for something.

Ali's father comes running out of the house with two men. They are carrying fire extinguishers. "Fire department is coming," one of them shouts, and they run across the lawn to my house. My house. To the den, the flickering den where my mother has blown herself up.

I grip the handlebars of my bike.

"Simone! Say something!" Ali shouts.

I think I might throw up. I feel upside down. The Page of Swords upside down, but it passes, and as soon as I seem right side up again, I get on my bike and pedal away from my house. Away from Ali and Sammy. My mother and Frank. An exhilaration builds up inside my rib cage. This is it. I'm gone!

The wind blows across my face, and I head out into the waiting night. Maybe I'll go home. To the city. I can smell fennel and the ocean, and something burning. Something burning.

Ali

"Where's she going?" Sammy asked me. We stood there stunned.

"She looks terrible," I said. "We'd better go after her."

"Do you think she started the fire?" he asked. "Do you think she's running?"

I stared at him. "No. Why would she do that?" We both looked over at the house. Black smoke was billowing now into the sky, looking pale in the darkness. We'd have to get her.

"Do you have a bike?" Sammy asked.

I nodded and ran to the shed on the side of the cottage. I rolled it out and he got on it.

"Wait a minute. You're not going without me." I slipped onto the crossbar in front of him. "All right, go!"

He didn't move. "There are hills out there," he told me.

"I'll run up the hills. Come on, she's getting away!"

Sammy pedaled out onto the road. We could barely see the flash of a reflector up ahead, and Sammy took off after her. "Where are the fire engines? Where are they?" I shouted.

"Volunteer," Sammy said. "They'll be here. Don't worry."

"Where do you think she's going?" I called to him once we couldn't see her anymore.

He was breathing hard. "I don't know. Does she know anybody? Where would she go?"

I shrugged, and flicked on the headlight that sent a weak beam of light out to bounce ahead of us in the darkness. We came to a hill and we both got off the bike and ran it up the incline. By the time we reached the top, we were both sweating and breathing hard. We stood in the intersection. Which way? Where had she gone?

Sammy stood very still. "I don't see anything. I don't hear anything. Where the hell would she go? You know her, Ali. Where do you think she'd go?"

Did I know her? Did I know anything about her at all? I thought for a minute. "To the ferry?" I guessed.

"Come on then." He opened his arm to me and I hopped on the bar again and we were off.

I knew we had to get Simone, had to bring her back, and yet I was worried about my father, who had run down the hill to the house with his two AA cronies. What if the fire department was too late? What if my father tried to put the fire out himself, or rescue anyone who was trapped inside? I shook my head fiercely to shake out the thoughts.

"Cripes!" Sammy shouted. "Sit still."

"Sorry." I'd concentrate on the ride. Up ahead through the trees we saw flashing red lights, and we could hear a siren now. When the truck came screaming up the hill at us, I shuddered uncontrollably. Sammy swerved, my extra weight throwing him off balance. He steered into the dirt on the side of the road and we were thrown from the bike. The fire engine flew past, then another, as we brushed ourselves off and righted the bike. My knee was scraped and stinging, blood running down my leg. Sammy's knuckles were scraped raw.

"Your turn," he said, handing the bike to me.

I stared at him blankly. "Come on," I said.

"What? What is this? You some kind of damsel in distress? I'm no white knight, you know."

"I've noticed," I muttered, staring down the road.

"Well? Aren't you liberated?" he taunted.

I glared at him. "If you were liberated of about fifty pounds you have over me, I might stand a chance."

"Get on," he said, surrendering. "But sit still, would you?"

"I'm trying, Sammy. Stop nagging."

"They should make this an Olympic event," he mumbled as I settled onto the crossbar and we headed back out onto the dark road. "Can't you see it? Riding doubles, up and down hills? That would be a real test of the men."

"Wait a minute," I said. "Why don't we try it with me sitting on the seat and you pedaling. Or I can sit on the back fender."

"There is no back fender," he said, turning to check it out. "How about the handlebars?" he asked. "I used to drive my brother that way."

"Me, sit on the handlebars?"

He was suddenly in love with the idea. "Yeah! Then the balance will be more evenly distributed. Come on." He pushed me from inside the circle of his arms and the handlegrips and steered me around to the front. I didn't dare shrink from this. I dug one foot onto the side wheel nut and hoisted myself onto the handlebars in front of him.

"Now sit still," he ordered.

"Sammy!"

And we were off, coasting down a slight incline, my hands holding on to the handlebars alongside me and my legs dangling on either side of the front wheel. The weak beam of the headlight shone on the road from between my legs. I felt as if I were a summer bug plastered to the front car of a roller coaster ride. I closed my eyes so I couldn't see the road flashing past beside me. Terror. Sheer terror. But Sammy drove steadily, with less complaining. I think I held my breath the entire time until I heard the ferry whistle. The ferry was leaving. I opened my eyes and the ferry dock area opened before me. The parking lot was empty and a couple of cars were on the ferry. The ferryman was pulling up the plank. I could see a girl's silhouette by the far railing, her bike standing alongside her. And for some reason I was desperately frightened for her. The ferry. The ferry. I thought of that little girl who once stood on the ferry like Simone was now.

"There she is! Wait!" Sammy screamed.

"Wait up!"

But the ferryman couldn't hear us. There was a long blast of the whistle, and the ferry did a slow pull away from the dock.

"Ah, we've missed it," Sammy said, slowing the bike, slamming his hand against the handlebar in disappointment. "And she's on it."

"We haven't missed it!" I shouted. As the bike slowed, I leaped off the front and ran faster than I'd ever run in my life. "Ali!" I heard Sammy call. The ferry was pulling away from the dock, the gap of water was widening, darkening, opening to me. I hit the edge of the dock with both feet and flew through the air. In midair I realized there was a gate across the back of the ferry. I hit it with my hands and held tight as I began to fall, slide down into the water. I felt my sandals slip off my feet, and dangling, clinging to the outside of the boat, I climbed my way up till my toes were wedged under the gate and I pulled myself over.

I heard Sammy whistling and cheering in the distance, but all I could think of was Simone. As I was climbing over the side, the ferryman was beside me.

"What the—"

"Sorry," I said, "I don't have a ticket, but this is really important—NO!" I screamed.

I could see Simone standing on the railing, balancing on both feet, like a tightrope walker. She held her arms out to her sides, and then just as I reached her, just as my hand was about to circle her ankle, she drew her arms in around her and stepped out into the churning horror of the black bay. Her bike crashed over beside me, and without thinking, I started to climb over the rail after her. The ferryman grabbed me by the shoulders to hold me back, but I flailed my arms at him, slapping, punching, and he lost his balance and fell over onto Simone's fallen bicycle. I dove headfirst into the water, filled with a fear that, like a wild chemistry experiment, had instantly transformed itself into some kind of courage.

"Simone!" I cried and choked. The water was dark and churning. I felt myself tossed and pulled, but I treaded water and bobbed, watching for her. Her head rose a distance away and I swam to her.

"Leave me be!" she screamed. "Leave me be!" I drew close, her face ugly now and distorted, her hair stringy and oily around her head. She flailed out at me. "Go away! Get away! Just let me die."

Suddenly the water was flooded with light. I heard the sound of the ferry engine cut off, and two fluorescent orange rings on ropes landed on either side of us.

"Come on, Simone," I said. "Nothing's that bad." I looped my arm through one of the rings, and with my other hand I tried to reach her. The current was pulling me, twisting me, making it hard for me to face her, as if a dozen little whirlpools were trying to spin me around. She stayed an arm's length away from me, crying, slapping at my hand that I held out to her.

"What do you know about it?" she screamed and sputtered. "You with your nice little picture-book family! With your studious little father and your studious little mother! What do you know about anything?"

The other glowing ring bobbed loosely beside her, slowly drifting away. I held my ring with all my strength, turning to it over and over to hold on with two hands, to secure my hold as the currents yanked at me. Then suddenly, like a fish breaking loose with my line and hook, the ring felt yielding and slack in my hand. The line had come loose from the ferry, and I heard men's voices yelling and hollering when my head broke the surface of the water.

"Simone!" I shouted. "Grab the line! Grab the line! Mine broke. I'm drifting out!" I was choking, slipping away from her, my legs exhausted, my arms aching and weak. I couldn't see her face, only the silhouette of her head with the ferryboat lights behind her. It seemed forever that she faced me in the water, almost still, almost as though something was holding her firmly while I was tossed around brutally, being pulled farther and farther away. "Simone! Please! Help me!"

I began to cry, and then I saw her turn to the second ring, the one that was still secured to the ferry. She slipped it over her shoulder and swam out to me. For an instant I had a vision of her swimming across her pool that first night, in the moonlight, when she was so annoyed that the water was too warm.

"So what do you think, Princess?" I said between chokes

and gasps. "A bit cooler than the pool, wouldn't you say?"

Simone reached out her hand to me without a word, and we clasped each other's wrists fiercely. I drew close to the ring and latched onto it, but I wouldn't let go of her wrist. I thought I'd never let go of her again. The churning bay tried to tug us out to some destiny we refused to meet, and the ferryman pulled us back to the ferry. Where we belonged. Simone and I held on to the ring and stared at each other.

The water rose over her face like a sheen as we cut through it, but she barely blinked her eyes, like some kind of mermaid. She just looked at me. Like she'd never seen me before.

"You okay?" I asked as we neared the side of the still ferry.

"You look pretty," she answered. And she turned to face the wall of the ferry's side and reached up to the dry hand that was held out to her. As Simone began to rise out of the water, I let go of her wrist at last, and as I did, I felt something snap under my hand, and dozens of yellow-pink shells from her promise bracelets showered down on my head. I watched as they disappeared all around me and sank into the dark water of the turbulent bay.

Then all was forgiven. Everything was clean.

Simone

It's nighttime, but you couldn't call it dark: The sky is splattered with light as if someone has thrown a bucket of stars across the universe. I can actually see the broad belt of the Milky Way, and the moon is a full fat egg, so bright it casts my shadow on the ground beside me. I sit here on a padded lounge and imagine I am on Dune Island, behind me the sloping lawns like the train of a royal cape, before me the bubbling dark waters of the pool, calling to me as sure and as clear as an invitation written on rich parchment.

But I wait, a medieval madonna here in the center of my island, the night sky peaking directly over my head. No one can tell where I end and where the night begins, where my skin stops and the darkness takes up. My legs are crossed like an ancient oracle's. My wrists balance on the crests of my knees and I wait. I meditate for the universe to send me my answers. A tightness slips over my throat like a sob, but I wait.

Thoughts of Adilia come to me now once again, thoughts of being very young, and sitting with her on a park bench, looking out at the water on the bay. I tell Dr. McAuley about Adilia during our talks. How I used to think that if I had tasted her, she would have tasted like gingerbread. Dr. McAuley laughed when I told her that. She would have liked Adilia, I know.

Tonight I remember sitting with Adilia by the bay and wanting to go home. It was time to leave, and I was restless, spoiled, but she had said, "We'll stay until a bird comes and tells us to go. Just wait now, chile." She slipped her arm around me and we stared out at the water together. Waiting. And soon, just as she had said, a swan appeared from nowhere and glided smoothly onto the center of the bay. Adilia had gotten up then, taken my hand, and led me home. I had felt so clear. So certain.

And now, the same. I wait. I close my eyes and imagine the house on Dune Island before me. There are no sounds. The king is sleeping. And the queen is passed out on the throne. The servants have gone for the night. Gradually I hear sounds, a car passing on the road, the ferry horn crying in the distance.

I sit motionless and wait for a sign to go on.

Ali

I hadn't been back to Simone's house since the night of the party. And I hadn't even been back at Dune Island for weeks, now that school had started again. It felt like a strange place with its cool, distant sun and the unfamiliar dune grass that had taken on a brushed golden color. As if I'd never been there before.

I walked along the peak of the property, seeing the Silvers' house down on my right and the bay down on my left. Lois ran ahead through the dunes to the water that was still so familiar to her, as if the late autumn made no difference.

Most of the windows on the blackened den of the Silvers' house were boarded up, but inside I could hear the hammering and noise of workmen. Two trucks were lined up in the driveway. I felt drawn to the house, to the den, wanting to walk around inside and see where it had happened. But I stood there on the crest, listening. Daddy told me Mrs. Silver had been free-basing cocaine, a special way to do it that makes it stronger, more powerful, and it had exploded, setting a sofa and other things into flames.

Mr. Silver had later confided to Daddy that she was in a special burn treatment center out west. But Sammy had heard that she was really in a drug treatment center upstate. Sammy had also heard that Frank had been with her. I didn't even ask Daddy about that one.

I never did leave and go back home early. I guess originally I had wanted to leave to get away from Simone. But then it just got more complicated than that. She stayed with us the night of the fire, up in the loft with me, and I tried to sleep, but every time I would look at her, she'd be lying there with her eyes wide open. Like she'd forgotten how to close them. She didn't speak to us; and when her father came, he told Daddy in whispers, and Daddy later told me in gentleness, that she was going to a special hospital, where she could rest and get some help. Seems Rebecca Silver's disease *had* hurt more than just herself after all. I felt different toward Simone, but I don't think I would have said I missed her.

I stayed around the rest of the summer making coffee for Daddy, biking, swimming; and Sammy and I hung out together. We even went water-skiing once with Brendan, but all the magic was gone from that, I can tell you. Actually he had skinnier legs than I like, and a weird laugh. So much for that sad love I had wanted at the beginning of the summer. Actually the sad part was leaving Sammy. Not that I loved him or anything. But it was funny. I never told him, never said a word, but one day before I left for home, we went into town for some ice cream and someone had written on the water tower, in big block letters with a spray can: ALI-CAT.

I smiled to think about it. I started down the crest to the bay. The hard wind tightened my jacket around me, and despite the cold, I had come barefoot, to feel the sand beneath my feet one more time. The blowing sand stung my ankles as I stumbled over the muffin-sized rocks, and then the shells, before coming close to the water. The sky billowed above me, and beneath my feet the damp sand turned so cold, my jaw ached. I didn't touch the water. Then I heard Lois barking and turned to look for her.

Up a ways on the beach, Lois danced around a young girl who held out her hand. I felt jolted inside. Simone. Dark hair blew around her face, and a large gray coat hung almost to her ankles.

"Lois!" I called. I almost called Simone, too, but I wasn't sure it was her. I began walking toward them, my eyes glued to her, and yet the closer I got, the more certain I was that this was not Simone. I was surprised at the disappointment that swelled up inside me, and the tears that clouded everything.

I bent over and clapped my hands against my thighs. "Lois! Get over here. Be a good girl!" Lois ran to my side and I held her close, patting her hollow ribs and burying my face and my unexpected tears for an instant in her golden fur.

"I love golden retrievers," a voice said, and I looked up and saw the young girl, a bright freckled face, hair now shades lighter than Simone's and a face a little younger than my own. I noticed the plastic bag she clutched in her hand. It was full of promise shells, and somehow it made me feel wise. Even a little cynical. "You live around here?" she asked.

"Not really," I said. "We rent a cottage up there, but we're only here in the summer and an occasional weekend, like now. How about you?"

"Yep. I live here. Inland a bit. My family's islanders since forever."

"How come I never saw you all summer?"

"I went to summer camp this year. Guess I missed you."

I motioned toward her bag of shells. "Making promise bracelets?" I asked.

She looked at me blankly.

"With your shells. Are you going to make bracelets out of them?"

She stared at them as if she'd never seen them before. "You know, I never thought of that. I'll bet they'd make really mint bracelets."

I was immediately sorry I'd told her. No one should make promise bracelets anymore. Maybe the secret could have died with me. "Well, what are you collecting them for?"

"Wind chimes," she told me.

"What's a wind chime supposed to do?" I asked.

"What do you mean?"

I felt impatient. "Well, does it bring you luck or do you make an oath on it, or do you hang it in your window and it calls back an old love?"

She smiled broadly at me and laughed. "No, you just put it on your porch or something, and it sounds nice and reminds you of the summer."

So simple, I thought. "How do you make them?"

She drew close. "Well, they have these tiny little holes here—"

"I know."

"—and you string maybe seven or eight of them, evenly knotted on a string, and hang them from a piece of driftwood, and then you do a whole bunch and hang it up. They bang up against each other and sound real pretty." She held out her arm as if one were hanging from her fingers already.

"That's nice," I said.

Lois' ears suddenly perked up and she stared back at the dunes. My father stood at the crest of the hill, his arm waving, his green scarf flicking in the wind. He whistled, and Lois scrambled after him.

"Lunch," I explained, "and then we're heading back west."

"Oh, but I just met you," she said, eager and disappointed.

"I'll be back once in a while." I walked backward away from her for a few steps, looking at her standing there with the bay behind her. She reminded me of myself. Of myself at the beginning of that summer. And I wasn't sure why.

The wind whipped more sand at me, stinging like needles along the backs of my feet and making me hold my arm up over my eyes. I turned to Daddy as he disappeared back toward the cottage.

"What's your name?" I heard her call over the wide-open roar of the bay wind.

"Alison!" I shouted. "Alison Mintz."

I turned back to the cottage and made my way up the dunes for the last time that year. At the top, I stopped and looked back at her. She was bending again over the strip of shells along the shore. "What's yours?" I called to her, but my voice was lost in the wind and carried out to sea, or maybe back over the Silver house.

The sky darkened as I stood there, and then light broke out in beams from the cold sky, sending dazzling light around the girl as she straightened up and looked out over the water. You know, for a minute there, with her standing so tall, and the light playing on the water, I could have sworn she looked like a princess. A fairy-tale princess.

I shook my head and turned my cold, damp feet back to the warmth of the cottage. No. For me, there'd always be only one princess of Dune Island. Only one.